B

# TROUBLE AT QUINN'S CROSSING

When Horatio Gill rode his wagon into Quinn's Crossing, few could have foreseen the load of trouble it carried. Horatio Gill, Grudden's Number One, was small but deadly, and the product he brought to Quinn's Crossing had spared many a range war.

But Gill's goal in life was to sell barbed wire and he didn't care what happened to the people he sold it to.

But Quinn's Crossing was a tight little town, and it was very questionable whether anyone would buy his wire.

More than likely they would hang him on it...

# TROUBLE AT QUINN'S CROSSING

## Nelson Nye

First published by Severn House 1978

This hardback edition 2000
by Chivers Press
by arrangement with
Golden West Literary Agency

ISBN 0 7540 8101 X

British Library Cataloguing in Publication Data available

Printed and bound in Great Britain by
Redwood Books, Trowbridge, Wiltshire

# I

Greenest eyes, whitest teeth and the reddest damn hair Horatio Gill had glimpsed in more months than he cared to think back on stood flatfooted in seven inches of water, and he hauled up the team for another look.

That she didn't much care for this was evident in the jut of that chin and the furious way her cheeks took fire, but Gill didn't let this spoil his enjoyment.

"Gracious!" he drawled with admiring enthusiasm. "Aren't you sort of pushing the season?"

The folded copy of a Tucson *Citizen* thrusting from a pocket of his rumpled coat bore a May 15 dateline, and she hadn't got on enough clothes to dust a fiddle.

"Ain't you never seen a woman before?"

She didn't look to have weathered more than seventeen summers but had obviously been at the front of the line when old Dame Nature was passing out the favors.

"Well, now," Gill said like he was searching his mind, "not bareass naked in the middle of a branch," and watched outraged eyes jerk away from his regard to throw a measuring scowl at flour sack drawers and faded cotton dress precariously shifting in the strengthening gusts swooping down off Bald Eagle. "Want I should fetch them for you?" he grinned.

"Don't you dast git out of that rig!"

"If this wind picks up," he observed with a chuckle, "in about ten seconds you'll be having to chase—"

With an infuriated snarl she lunged for the bank, snatched up the fluttering garments and, whirling, glared with them hugged to the front of her. "Confound you!" she cried. "You figgerin' to set there and watch me git into them?"

Before Gill could dredge up an answer to that, something ripped into the side of his wagon like the kick of a mule, the crash swallowed up in the blast of a rifle.

5

He ducked like a dude. Very fast to react, without waiting for an encore Gill grabbed loose the whip and, applying it with vigor, sent the team through the water in a wild churn of wheels.

With his matched pair of bays lunging into their collars he went clattering up the grade at the crossing's far side with every last ounce of speed he could shake out of them. Nor did he pause to look back, beyond a glance at his load to make sure he still had it, till he was comfortably behind a bend in the bluff. At which time, gasping a bit to get hold of his breath, he dropped the team into a walk while he wiped the cold sweat off the back of his neck.

In the course of a somewhat hectic career he'd come up against some fairly rough people—not a few with prejudices quite as violent as this.

If you must have it honest, they were his favorite kind. But, while he'd acquired no little skill in the patterns of survival, he'd never been one to risk profitless chances and this redheaded filly appeared to stand in that category.

Putting her out of mind, he drove on with the jaws of the mountains swiftly closing him in, somberly rising at both sides of the road. Instead of being lost, the sound of the creek left behind in the canyon became increasingly loud, growing into a roar as—rounding a second sharp twist in the grade—he found the road crawling beneath the barrier rim of a two hundred foot cliff.

Centered up there was one clear break, maybe twenty feet wide, out of which poured with a white, rushing turbulence the source of the water that girl had been standing in. Alongside this break ran the road, roughly climbing.

Considering the load, it looked a pretty fierce pull.

But there were buildings up there. He could glimpse chimney smoke and the back ends of some of them, and where there were buildings you generally found people.

A community of interests was what founded towns, and where there were towns there was bound to be trade. For Gill's brand of wares these isolated places at the back of beyond offered prospects far exceeding possibilities normally encountered in more bustling marts of commerce.

In such tiny, tucked away hamlets there were a lot less controls, more opportunities for angers to fester, and angers were Gill's greatest source of profit. Most men in his line, not that these were in large supply, tended to work the farming centers, the orchard communities, the places where risk was pared down to a minimum. But Gill had discovered the commissions ran larger where men ran cattle, once you'd got through the red tape of prejudice. And that was faster got done with in regions like this, dominated mostly by one or two outfits, the bitter rest hanging on by no more than a toenail.

He pulled up and got down to check with some thoroughness the weight riding lashed under cover of the tarp. Satisfied there had been little shifting, the load reasonably secure, he climbed back to the seat and unwrapped the lines, pausing just a bit longer for another look round.

This wariness was habitual with him, and sometimes he had thought in more depressed moments if a man had to get out and drum up business he would be better off in corsets or bustles. In *his* line of trade a man made few friends and multitudinous enemies, some of these more than just a bit deadly, and all of them with memories and an aptitude for popping up in damned unlikely places.

He was in a dangerous business but the take was big and increasing steadily; and for a man like Gill with a nose for profits, no other line appeared half as rewarding. There were worse things than winding up dead with your boots on, and no need of that where a man kept his eyes peeled.

He shook out the lines and clucked to his horses.

Above the falls—when Gill at last got his outfit up there—what he actually found was not greatly different than what, from below, he'd been led to anticipate. A handful of houses little better than shacks squatted like chicks round a great mother hen of a barnlike structure with the legend QUINN'S CROSSING daubed across its front in red painted letters nearly two feet high.

What he hadn't thought to see was that line of hitched saddlers switching flies at the tie rails. Eighteen he counted, and reckoned from experience this had to be a payday for the cattle spreads using Quinn's Crossing for a point of supply.

The largest number, he noted, looking over the brands,

seven, to be exact, were in an iron whose mark most resembled a sunburst. Four were branded Bar 7; two Lazy S. The rest were all different, probably one-man spreads living from hand to mouth on beef purloined from more affluent neighbors—a situation well suited to make the most of Gill's talents.

Driving off to one side he got out of the wagon, anchoring his team with a pair of iron weights snapped to their cheekstraps. After which, with covert stare still probing his surroundings, he leisurely stretched to flex the cramps from tired muscles. Cuffing trail dust from the town suit covering his five foot ten frame, Gill took his range man's scrinch-eyed face toward the wide open doors of the place where the action was.

He was scarcely ten feet short of the entrance when a burly customer, staggering out of the place grumbling under his breath in a surly growl, abruptly pulled up to blink surprised eyes with his red-veined stare gloweringly traveling from Gill to the wagon.

"Nice day," Gill nodded, stepping out of his way.

"Who the hell are you?" the man demanded with glaring belligerence.

Gill said, "Just a lost wagon merchant hunting a rail to prop his best foot on."

Still scowling, the man, with a snort, wallowed off toward the horse line, grumbling obscenities when a lifted foot kept missing the stirrup as he tried to board a flea-bitten gray carrying the mark of Barred Circle.

Gill, not waiting to see if he made it, stepping carefully round, passed through the open doors into a pungent aroma compounded of barreled sorghum, rotgut, saddle leather, sweat and the good smell of mingled spices and java. There were no other customers in this general store section of the barnlike building, but the fattest man Gill had seen in a coon's age sat fanning himself in a huge homemade chair just back of the nearest counter.

He had on bib overalls, faded and patched, with hooded eyes nearly shut as he followed the raucous gabble of talk welling through louvered doors beneath a shaving brush sign spelling out the word BAR.

Gill tipped him a nod. "Sounds like you got a fight building up."

The fat man grunted. "All bristle an' snarl."

He was bald as a monk with a fringe of black fuzz before and behind a pair of jug handle ears with long hairs curling out of them. A boiled shirt that probably once had been white was collar buttoned together beneath the layers of flesh quivering under his jaws at each swing of the hand that was stirring the air with an H. Kauffman & Sons leather goods catalogue.

"Pretty dry," Gill mentioned. "How's the water situation?"

The man's puffy lids jerked up and down and the little pig eyes squinted fractionally at Gill while he heaved his bulk to a more comfortable position. "Depends who you ask. It ain't botherin' Del Sol that I've been able to notice." He sucked air through his teeth. "If you're huntin' a job, you're in the wrong place."

"What's the chances of getting put up for the night?"

"Is that cash money talkin'?"

"I could probably scrape up some if the accommodations suit."

"For bed an' board I git five dollars a night."

"I've got a wagon outside and a team to be fed."

The fat man's stare showed a flicker of interest. "That'll be extry. You reckon to roost here for long?"

Gill grinned at him, chuckling. "I don't aim to bust sod if that's what you're driving at."

"You ain't got the look of a drummer."

"They all look alike?" Gill asked with a smile.

The man in the chair continued to peer, while he mopped at his chins with a wrinkled bandanna. "Could be some in these part will lay odds you're one of them bounty hunters—"

"Not when they learn what I've got in that wagon." Extracting a flossy card from his wallet, Gill set it down on the counter, the fat man watching from those half-covered eyes.

"Horatio Gill," he read, spelling it out. Then his stare, suddenly sharpening, leaped to Gill's face. "You'll sell none of that here!"

Gill spread his hands. "Time'll tell."

"Last feller tried it damn near got lynched. Folks around here believe in free grass."

Gill thought of several pungent answers he could have come up with but left them unsaid to throw out a bit of bait he'd found helpful before when working a pitch in unfriendly territory. "As the storekeeper here you're entitled to ten percent of any sales I make. And you don't have to stock it or step into any risk."

"I don't aim to. You can get that part of it straight right now."

They looked at each other for several moments while the growls and angry bickering from the bar grew more obstreperous. The fat man, swabbing at his chins again, grudgingly said, "You're not payin' out commissions without expectin' something for 'em."

"Well," Gill mentioned, "that ten percent is mostly for good will, but I'm going to need something to hang the stuff on. I want to build a corral and if you'll furnish the posts I'll up that another two cents on the dollar."

"How big a pen you figurin' to put up?"

"A kind of bull ring's what I've really got in mind. For diameter . . . say about two hundred yards. And if I can build it on your water right, the corral will be yours—plumb free of charge—soon's I get done with it."

He said after a moment, "You're not dealing with any fly-by-night outfit—Mister . . . ?"

"Quarls—Dutch Quarls."

"Thank you. I've got this all down in writing, Mr. Quarls," Gill said, producing a printed form from his coat's inside pocket and holding it out.

The fat man, putting on a pair of spectacles, read it, and after reading it again sat a spell in frowning silence, eyeing Gill suspiciously. "What's the idear?" he grumbled, tapping the paper.

"A mere formality, just a way of making certain we both know where we stand. Company policy. Wouldn't want any cause for hard feelings now, would we?"

Quarls sniffed, and his fish belly stare dug into Gill harder. "I'm not signin' no goddamn papers."

Gill shrugged again. "Your word's good with me, but them brass collar dogs settin' back in Chicago don't know you from Adam, Mr. Quarls. They don't want no bills for posts coming at 'em. If you're not willing to show good faith by putting your name on that dotted line, reckon I'll just plain have to look elsewhere."

"Much good that'll do you.

"Well, you never can tell," Gill said, reaching out for his paper. "This wire has its uses, and if water's got short as it looks in this country one of your neighbors . . ."

"Hold on!" Quarls growled, dropping onto the paper a fist that looked like a bunch of bananas. "What gives you that notion?"

"I've got pretty good ears," Gill smiled, inclining his head toward the racket from the bar. "That Del Sol feller—"

"Ain't a feller. It's a outfit. Hacienda del Sol . . ."

"Gracious!" Gill exclaimed as though Quarls had told him he'd just been written into somebody's will. "My company has a first rate affinity for that kind of spread—they purely have! Think of those miles and miles of good stout wire a really big outfit could use. Lordy me! In a time of trouble there's few things as comforting as knowing you're covered with the good solid security of Grudden's barbed wire. Have you heard of our motto? 'No job too big. By the foot or carload three strands of—' "

A man burst through the bar's louvered batwings like a dog taking off with a can on its tail. He cried, glaring round, "You hear that, Dutch? This goddamn Rivas has just give out *any critter not packin' the Del Sol brand found using Middle Water will be shot on the spot!* Who the jumpin' Jesus does he think he is?"

## II

RAWBONED AND GANGLING, the man in his turmoil banged a fist down so hard everything on the counter rattled and stood on the brink of departure. "By God," he swore, "we'll see about that! No chile eatin' hog of a duded up Mex is goin' to tell *us* where to git off at!"

Red-necked and freckled, he had the look of a man from the piney wood hills with the steel trap mouth of a lantern jaw, so compressed with his outrage it was a wonder, Gill thought, he didn't just plain go straight up in smoke. He couldn't stand still, so volatile was the fury inside him. With another wild shout, he tore out of the place like Sheridan trying to come up with Sherman.

"Well!" Gill said. "You got many like him?"

Quarls swabbed at his chins with the limp bandanna, looking pretty unsettled for a man without wrinkles. "Got a right to be riled if he can't get to water. Foreman he is for Hallie Crockett—her that owns Bar 7, with her daddy just buried six days ago yesterday. Been sharing that water with Del Sol for years—runs between both outfits, bend of the Santa Cruz, belongin' to neither. But—" he puffed out his cheeks, "Rivas, I reckon if he puts his mind to it, is just about big enough to gobble it all."

"What about the rest of 'em, the small spreads around here?"

"It's them," Quarls said glumly, "I reckon he's after. Been a mort of maverickin' these last couple years. Rivas wanted old Crockett to help run 'em out but he never would do it. Trash, Rivas calls them, rustlers an' worse. Appears like he's finally took the bit in his teeth."

Gill scratched at an ear and shook his head. You wouldn't hardly think that here was a man who made his living off violence. Presently rousing, he said piously, "Feller sure hates to see things of that sort let loose on a place. Be an open invitation to every hard case hears of it."

Quarls heaved a sigh. "Country's 'bout dry enough to plumb blow away, an' with everyone's temper on a short fuse . . ."

"Thought from your tell 'twas all bristle and snarl."

"That was before. With all these folks shut away from that water . . . Well!" He rubbed at his cheeks. "You heard Reb Lockhart."

"Lockhart's boss is a woman."

"Girl," Quarls said. "Old man married late. Citified woman —couldn't keep hold of her. Run off with a coffee drummer."

"How big's that outfit?"

"Run—or been runnin'—some three, four hundred head of mother cows."

"And Del Sol?"

"Don't reckon they've ever got around to halfway count-in'. 'Bout every second critter you'll see is packin' Rivas's brand."

"Still and all," Gill smiled, seeming more pleased than otherwise, "this Crockett girl . . . she ain't redheaded is she?"

"No," Quarls said shortly, on the tail of a sharpened look.

"Still," Gill pronounced, going on with his thought, "this dame is the owner and not a heap likely to want to lock horns—"

"If you reckon any filly still wet behind the ears is goin' to keep the likes of Reb Lockhart in line, you better lay off to git bored for the simples! One of his kin was killed at the Alamo, an' none of his folks has ever forgot it. Feller's been itchin' ever since he come in here to find some excuse for tanglin' with Rivas."

Gill said, thoughtfully peering toward the bar, "Rivas in there now?"

The fat man nodded, still rummaging Gill's face.

"Hmm. Better see what I can do," Grudden's wagon merchant muttered, after chewing on his lip. "An outsider, maybe, might just come up with something that would make sense to him . . . more, anyhow, than the kind of corpse and cartridge affair he's going to kick off if he starts shooting cattle."

With this laudable notion he pushed through the batwings.

The place seemed a lot less crowded than that line of hitched ponies had led him to expect. But, counting barman and customers, and the deadbeats nursing empty glasses at the tables, Gill reckoned he had enough within earshot to be sure what was said would get prompt circulation.

He'd no trouble picking Rivas out of this assemblage. The man stood out among these misfits like a fresh painted barber's pole against a drift of snow.

He was handsome enough, with that toothbrush mustache above the white flash of teeth, as he stood regarding a sawed-off professorial type in rusty Prince Albert and steel-rimmed cheaters, behind which his myopic stare appeared about as disbelieving as Foxy Loxy probably looked after listening to Chicken Little. "Surely you can't seriously

13

imagine," he was saying in shocked tones, "you can go around slaughtering cattle with impunity!"

The hard looks he was getting didn't bother Rivas any. He was in that physical muscular prime that pushes a man into saying what he thinks without regard to any possible hereafter. "If you don't want them shot you better keep your cows to home, Sneed."

The bespectacled man, affronted, said, "You sound like something straight out of the Dark Ages. This is free range, Rivas."

Rivas laughed. "Let me tell you something, Sneed. Nothing's really free in this world once you've brushed aside all the bushes. Only rights a man has are those he's big enough to glom onto. If you don't believe that, you're in for tough sleddin'. Don't try to tell *me* about this country—I was here before you Yanks ever heard of it!"

While Sneed stood spluttering, Gill, moving forward, made a place with blunt elbows alongside of Rivas. "Ain't you from Del Sol? My name's Gill. Something I've got in my wagon might interest you."

The olive-skinned cowman whipped a stare over him not many would take unless it came from their wives; but Gill jerked a nod, "Sure cure for your problems."

He fished in a pocket, laid a hand on the bar and left beside the man's glass a three-inch strand of Grudden's barbed product. "Straight from our coffee mill," he said, grinning.

"Devil wire!" Rivas swore, looking half-minded to take a swing at him.

"Finest fence in the world," Gill smilingly assured him. "Light as air. Stronger than whiskey and cheaper than dirt. And, what is more, no goddamn cow ever weaned can get through it."

All ears pricked up on those canted heads, as men hitched forward the better to hear, but Rivas, with no more change than you'd get from a plugged nickel, coldly said, "Talk's cheap. Takes hard cash to buy good whiskey."

"You're certainly right about that," Gill agreed and, solemn as a judge but with real showman flourish, laid a ten dollar gold piece flat on the bar. "Fill 'em up all around," he bade the apron and, peering hard at Rivas, said: "We're not talking about shoddy substitutes now. Proof of the pudding generally comes with the eating, so here's what I'll do. Right out of my pocket I'll put up a corral with three strands of this stuff and ten days from now you fetch in some steers—biggest, raunchiest, toughest you've got—and if this wire don't hold 'em, you've got five hundred dollars for every one that gets through."

Now the longhorn steer in that country and time was nothing to pick up a boot and yell *Boo!* at. He was the world's roughest breed, a dynamo of energy, and every bit as contrary as a young widow woman after her fifth husband's funeral.

But the sly amusement in that mahogany face through the gasps that greeted this brash proposal did not put Gill a whit off his stride. "You heard right," he nodded. "Five hundred smackers for every brute that gets through. Are you on, Mr. Rivas, or did you open your mouth just to hear your head rattle?"

Rivas's face darkened, but with so many of these despised two-bit neighbors, staring openmouthed, taking in every maddening nuance of this scene he compromised with impulse sufficiently to growl, "What the hell will that prove?"

"It'll prove, for one thing, you don't have to shoot cattle to keep 'em out of your hair," Gill grinned back at him coolly. And, now that he'd got this far with his scheme, proceeded with devastating aplomb to sink and firmly seat the gaff.

"Five hundred bucks for each and every steer that gets loose. But if this wire holds 'em, you on your part," he proclaimed, tapping Rivas on the chest, "hereby agree and make covenant to engage my time and services to string whatever amount of this wire you figure it'll take to fence outside cattle away from that water."

### III

THE BESPECTACLED Sneed, observing Rivas's discomfort, loosed a spiteful laugh and, thus emboldened, three or four others snickered, while the flush crept again above the cattleman's collar.

Griped right down to the spurs on his boots, he snarled,

scowling round: "Be a whole heap cheaper to shoot the goddamn critters!"

"Well . . . gracious! Guess that's up to you, Mr. Rivas, but in the course of my experience I've found few bullets ever stopped to consider what sort of meat they was being shoved into. Flesh and bone ain't rightly a thing a man ought to trifle with."

Rivas's fiercening stare turned downright ugly as the ramifications in this took hold of him, and some of the subtler aspects of the message began to sift through the throes of his anger.

He arched his back like a stubborn mule but was shrewd enough to realize the drawling stranger had managed to rope him into something he couldn't back out of. Caught hard and fast in this web of duplicity, pride demanded he take up the challenge and he grudgingly said, like the screak of a gate badly in need of oil, "I'll be here," and stomped from the place, his crew trailing after him.

In the growth of silence following their departure, Gill observed that most of the hombres still clutching his largess were uneasily watching the sweat-streaked face of a burly buck with one bent over ear, who, in slovenly range clothes—shirt open to navel across hairy chest—stood scowling into his whiskey like some kind of helgramite was taking a swim in it.

"Shit!" this fellow said, shifting his wad across tobacco-stained teeth to pull up his head with a hard look around which he dropped on Gill when no one else would meet it. "Shit!" he said again, and emptying the glass at one gulp slammed it into a corner and stalked through the batwings with a belligerent sneer.

Until his boots crossed the porch and faded somewhere beyond, no one around Gill moved or said anything. No one looked his way either till, finishing his own drink, he said brightly, "Gracious! Guess that must be Mr. Big around here"; after which, the whole bunch appeared to reach for new breath.

"Bad medicine, that Jingo," Sneed grudgingly muttered; and another, standing next to him, grumbled, "Plumb crazy."

"Work for Rivas, does he?"

The second speaker shrugged and Sneed, with a covert

glance of those myopic eyes, mumbled, "Nobody knows *what* he does for a living. When they've got any choice, folks stay out of his way," and, tugging his hat firmly down round his ears, he, too, departed.

After another ten minutes squandered in the hope of hearing something to his advantage, Gill picked up his change and drifted out of the bar, discovering that Quarls, in the store part of his establishment, had been favored with a customer, a rawboned, old biddy in a buckskin skirt and a man's sun-greened hat with a pinned back brim, who kept barking out orders as if she were buying for a regiment.

Quarls's robust butt was still warming his chair, while the redheaded girl Gill had seen in the river hopped around like a cricket getting things off the shelves for this crotchety customer. Since the shelves went all the way up to the ceiling she was frequently compelled to mount a ladder on rollers, a feat Gill followed with considerable interest, no whit abashed by the looks she threw at him.

The fat man, scowling, presently said, "Somethin' you wanted, Gill?"

"I ain't in no hurry."

Lounging with hip on the ironbound rim of an open cracker barrel, he continued to munch on occasional samples till Quarls testily asked, "Don't you want a mite of cheese with them fixin's?"

"Gracious!" Gill left off his ogling to level a glance of mild reproach at the man. "Considering the moolah I just dropped in your bar a bit of free lunch don't appear unreasonably exorbitant. Not to mention the corral I'm about to build you for free."

"You mean—" Quarls looked astonished, "Rivas ackshully made some kind of deal with you?"

"He not only made it, he's furnishing the steers. Ten days from now he's committed to give that wire a workout. He reckons to fatten his bank account by five hundred smackers for every steer that gets loose. But if my wire holds 'em," Gill spoke with relish, "he's engaged to pay for enough more and services to fence outside stock plumb away from that water."

Quarls shook his head.

In a pitying voice, he told the wire salesman, "Hope springs eternal. You're hooked either way, boy."

"You tryin' to say he won't buy that fence?"

"He'll buy it, all right, if that dratted wire holds them. But when you come for your pay he'll just laugh in your face."

"Says you!"

"That's right. You better quit while you're ahead."

Gill scowled at the patronizing look on Quarls's face. "You just get them posts ready, handsome. Anyone thinks he's going to welsh on me better take another squint at his high card."

Despite this assurance, Gill's tightened mouth gave the impression he was not as happy in his mind as he had been. "You probably won't take it," the fat man said, "but for whatever it's worth my advice to you is hitch up your wagon an' hit for someplace where the law takes care of delinquent debtors."

"You get out them posts. I'll handle Mr. Rivas."

"With the kind of crew Del Sol has on its payroll you'll be lucky even to *see* him once that fence is finished. An' that," Quarls said, "just ain't the half of it. You shut these small spreads away from that water, you could wake up bein' rode out of here in a coat of hot tar an' feathers!"

"Hoo hoo!" Gill jeered, though with something less than his former confidence. For if there was a vestige of truth in Quarls's words, and Rivas reneged when the time came for payment, he could look pretty foolish after working his tail off. He said, "By God, we'll cross that pole when we come to it!" and went out to look after his horses.

He slept pretty well the next couple of nights, despite the wrench Quarls had dropped in his prospects; but the following morning with no posts on hand and some of the locals beginning to lay bets there would be no fence when the Del Sol crew brought in Rivas's steers, Gill went hunting the fat man with blood in his eye.

"Mr. Quarls is not here," the redhead told him when Gill came striding into the store.

"Where the Sam Hill are them fenceposts he promised?"

"I know nothing of that."

Glaring, he went charging into the bar but no one was there, neither loafers nor apron. Cursing and fuming he shoved back through the batwings. "Where *is* that fat slob?"

All the answer she gave him to that was a shrug.

"You live here, don't you?"

"What's that got to do with it?"

"If you sleep with— *Hey!* Jumpin' jehosaphat!" Gill yelled, ducking, as a flung tin narrowly missed his head. "What—"

"I put up with plenty! I don't have to take that! I sleep with myself and *you better believe it!*" she snapped, appearing angry enough to clobber him. "Now git, an' quick, before I forget I was raised up a Christian!"

Resentment became her, but Gill thought better of his impulse to say so. Dragging off his hat, he was about to dredge up not an apology exactly but something calculated at least to ease her across this hump of stirred temper. He had hardly opened his mouth before, with the jerk of a hand toward the street, she cried: *"Git!"*

"I'm going," he yelped as she twisted toward a rack of iron skillets. He didn't quite run but he sure didn't dawdle to hunt any posies.

Outside, peering round for something to kick, he saw a just arrived buggy, with reins round the whipstock, in imminent danger of overturning as the mogul of Quinn's Crossing, with a deal of wheezing and sundry grunts, attempted to extricate himself from the vehicle.

"Gill—" he puffed, beckoning. "Come over and hold this contraption still, will you?"

"Where are them posts?" Gill growled, standing pat, watching Quarls hang—as they say in the Navy—betwixt wind and water.

"They're comin'. I've just been to see about 'em; no cause to—"

"When?"

"If you'll git me outa this thing, I'll tell you!"

"Tell me now," Gill demanded, thumbs hooked in his galluses.

The buggy groaned like a rusty gate as Quarls with braced hands nervously twisted his head to fetch Gill into a more exact focus, the sweat standing out like great shiny beads on the quivering sag of those shaved hog jowls. He looked pretty desperate as he cried with the bleat of a frightened sheep: "Have you no compunction at all?"

"When a man's doing business with a bunch of Philistines he'd have to be all fired soft in the head—"

"All right," Quarls wailed, "they'll be here this evenin'. Now git me outa this goddamn thing!"

The buggy collapsed with a squeal of racked springs while the sauntering Gill was yet three strides away. But he dived for the horse as it started to rear and, with the animal back on a firm foundation, peered round through the dust to see if its driver was still in one piece.

He was there, right enough; this fact attested to by the piteous moans rising out of the wreckage. Unhitching the horse while he swore at it soothingly, Gill finally got round to attending to its owner, even gave him a hand in real Samaritan fashion, but had to use both to get Quarls onto his feet. Except for some scrapes and possible bruising the man didn't appear to be very much hurt, but there was no getting round the state of his mind.

He spoke it plainly, knocking aside Gill's gallant attempt to brush some of the dirt off his disheveled clothing. "Git away!" he snarled meanly. "Don't touch me!" he cursed. "An' keep your damn paws off that girl, too—you hear me?"

Gill stepped back, straightening. "*What* girl?" he said as though wondering if Quarls had lost some of his marbles.

"How many you think I got workin' here? Jude Jackson, that's *who!* I've seen how she looks at you! She's bound by the courts an' got five years t' go so don't fill her head with no sweet-talkin' nonsense!"

## IV

A BOUND GIRL, by God! In *this* day and age!

Gill, sitting after supper in the half-lit bar glumly nursing a flat beer, kept pushing it around like a dog with a bone, at a loss to imagine how a looker like her had been caught in such a bind. And he wondered how much of the fat man's tale was tailored before it got past his teeth.

It was the apron's night off and she was taking his shift behind the mahogany, self-consciously ruffled and beginning to bristle under the persistence of Gill's probing scrutiny. Save for these two the place was deserted with Quarls off somewhere pampering his bruises. "Don't you ever," Gill said, "get fed up with this?"

The puzzled look on her cheeks made him say irritably, "Playing slavery, I mean, to that outsized hypothecator!"

"How else would I keep a roof—"

"Oughta be younger gents in these parts would be happy enough to take care of that for you—ain't all of 'em blind, are they?"

A deepening color surged into her face above the glass she was shining. She gave him a straight look. "I expect you mean well," she spoke thoughtfully, "but bound to Quarls I'm not at the moment rightly fixed to entertain offers of marriage."

It was Gill's turn to flush. Staring, aghast, "Hell!" he said, and you'd have thought the way he got out of that chair a scorpion had found its way up his pants leg. "Nobody's about to get *me* in double harness! I wouldn't crawl into that with *no* dratted female!" And he curled back his lips to explode with a snarl, "Not, by God, if she come with her pockets crammed with diamonds an' pearls!"

And he got out of that bar like the heel flies were chasing him.

He didn't get much rest in his bunk that night, what with turning and twisting and the sweat pouring out of him; nor was all of this restiveness due entirely to heat. Buckling his shell belt he was out on the street a good half hour ahead of the sun, pretty seriously thinking of hauling his freight.

But when a man gets his teeth sunk into a thing, he is loath to abandon it; and the way Gill had this community sized up, all the rest of the prospects appeared too rosy to let any dang filly stand in his way.

A brace of teamsters heading for the bar to settle their breakfasts each took a hard squint and got off the walk with a show of alacrity you wouldn't expect from the rough sort of gents in their line of work.

Peering over their shoulders as Gill strode past, the one worst in need of a shave told the other, "What d'you reckon is chewin' on him?" and his companion, turned paler, growled

21

under his breath, "If I hadn't of seen the sonofabitch planted I'd give you odds that was—"

"Shh! He's comin' back!"

"You fellers lookin' for work?"

The skinny snaggletoothed one, looking much as he might had the devil accosted him, shook his head emphatically; but the burly one, Harry, tone hedged in bluster, said, "What kinda work?"

"Setting posts."

"What's it pay?"

"Two bucks a day plus grub and protection."

Snaggletooth's apple bobbed when that last word came out. The whiskered one said, "What do we have to be protected against?"

"Nothing, probably. I chucked that in just in case."

The big teamster, pawing at his cheeks, finally grumbled, "It ain't that I wouldn't like t' seem more obligin', but to tell you the truth—with my back like it is—I expect my ol' woman . . . Guess you better hunt you up someone else." And, without more ado, he took after his companion who had already vanished inside Quarls's establishment.

On a sudden thought, Gill headed for the livery and there, sure enough, he found the wagons, still loaded. "When'd them posts get here?" he demanded, rousting out the hostler.

"Come in last night."

"For Quarls?"

"That's right." The man, sizing him up, said, "You figgerin' to tear into 'em straight off? Before breakfast?"

"If I can't get nobody else to. Look—I'll pay two dollars—"

The stableman laughed. "Better roll up yer sleeves. Won't nobody round here touch 'em fer that."

"Why not? Who else in this country will pay—"

"No one, I reckon. Tell you one thing, Mac. I wouldn't do it fer five times that much—not with Mike Rivas lookin' down my throat!"

"What's Rivas got to do with it?"

"Stick around long enough an' you'll likely find out," the fellow tossed over a shoulder as he went back inside.

Gill, with clenched jaws and a pugnacious stride, sailed into Quarls's place and on through the batwings like Moses about to pass round the tablets. The fat man—himself behind the bar for a change—chucked the wire peddler a stare, as Gill hove to some five or six inches behind burly Harry. "Ain't you sort of forget something, buster?"

The snaggletoothed one, eyeing Gill's reflection, visibly shuddered as his bigger companion set down his glass to bunch muscled shoulders like a sore-backed bull about to paw up some sod.

But just about then something hardly round and considerably rigid thumped the man's spinal column. There was force enough behind this prod to jam shocked ribs flat against the bar. Gill said in clipped tone, "Go hook up your teams and fetch them posts to the front of this dive and get 'em unloaded."

"Now see here—" Harry blustered.

"You heard me. Get moving!"

Harry, doubling both fists, shoved himself off the bar. But as he whirled, swinging wildly, Gill's six-shooter took him alongside the head and he went down for the count.

With a hard look at Harry's blanch-faced companion, Gill stepped round the bar and, shoving Quarls out of his path, picked up the bucket used to rinse dirty glasses and upended the contents where it would do the most good.

Harry, spluttering and gasping, came onto one knee looking like a drowned rat. While he was still endeavoring to recapture his wind Gill softly said: "You got just thirty minutes to empty both wagons, and if you want to stay healthy you better get at it."

"Just a second," Quarls interposed, leaning over his bar. "I don't want that corral—"

"Sorry, Charlie. You already signed for it."

"Not smack in front of my store!" wailed Quarls.

"Paper doesn't even mention your store. What it says is you grant, all legal and binding, my company the right to build at its option *on posts to be furnished* five hundred foot of fence with Grudden's barbed wire . . . on your water right. Only water I see runs in *front* of your establishment. Maybe you better have yourself another look."

The fat man's jaws came together with a snap that couldn't have done his dentures much good. The color of his stare gave ample indication Horatio Gill had him where the hair was shortest.

Though his eyes winnowed down to glittering slits, what he read in Gill's face put a hobble on his lip and he watched in a smoldering silence as Gill trailed the teamsters out onto the street.

Lounging in the shade of Quarls's wooden awning, Grudden's energetic rep slouched with crossed arms against one of the porch posts chewing a toothpick while the disgruntled pair hoofed it back to the livery. He took a look at his timepiece after standing there a bit and, when a further five minutes slipped past without action, was about to go legging it up the street himself when the first of the wagons wheeled into sight.

The snaggletoothed driver pulled up ten feet away. "This where you want 'em?"

"Anyplace there. Just get 'em rolled off it."

While the fellow was sweating the stakes from the load Harry, still scowling, fetched up the second wagon. Gill, eyeing his watch, said, "Ten minutes to go."

It was the fastest unloading ever seen at Quinn's Crossing.

When the last post banged down and the sweat streaked pair were mopping their faces, Gill casually said, laying out a rough circle, "Here's where she goes. A post every twelve feet. You can get your tools from Quarls."

Out of a tight-mouthed, astonished silence the big-shouldered Harry, about half ready to slam down his hat, said *"Tools!"* with a mean-tempered, hard-eyed snarl.

"Whatever you need."

*"I* don't need a goddamn thing!"

"Well, I never been one to push a man none, but you'll look mighty puny trying to dig holes—"

"I ain't diggin' no holes!" The furious Harry scrinched up his mouth to give all and sundry a piece of his mind when the sober-faced Gill, never glancing at either of them, lifted the six-shooter off his thigh.

Swinging out the cylinder he give it a twirl, peered through the barrel and flicked the gate shut to look up amusedly as both pair of boots made a rush for the porch, drumming across it to dive through Quarls's door.

Tossing the pistol and dexterously palming it Gill stepped

off to catch a clear view of the bar's side door exit. Just as it began to swing furtively open, he sent three slugs crashing into the lintel.

"Digging time, boys. Grab up them tools and let's get the rag out."

## V

HE LET THEM knock off at noon to replenish their energy, allowing them scarcely half an hour, sitting there watching with grunts of impatience each time a fork appeared likely to pause in the course of its journey between plate and mouth. As Harry said later while out of Gill's hearing: "That sonofabitch, if you give him a whip, could pass anyplace for Simon Legree!"

By midafternoon, during the worst of the heat, considerable of a crowd had taken up stations in the shade of Quarls's porch to offer boisterous gems of unsolicited advice to the shirtless diggers each time Gill stepped into the bar to affix a new collar to his mug of warm beer.

Returning from one such trip, Grudden's drummer descried among the assemblage a pair of faces not previously noted. One was Lockhart's—the Bar 7 boss; the second he hitched to the cauliflower-eared hombre Sneed had called "Jingo." With a hard, reckless smirk of tobacco-stained teeth the latter folded bare arms and spat as Gill passed.

That Gill chose not to make an issue of this may have fostered an impression that would not stand up to the close probing scrutiny it got from the spitter—not that Gill gave a damn what *any* of them thought. He was here to sell wire, and the only fool thing he could not abide was a notion or act which might tend to prevent him. Anything else he could shrug off or laugh at. Tipping a grin at the Bar 7 ramrod, he sat down again and took a pull at his beer.

If the blue of Jingo's skimmed milk stare bothered him, no evidence of this was even vaguely discernible. The thinking part of him was taken up mostly with trying to work out some system of dodges which might utilize Lockhart's ingrained prejudice to hang wire, too, around Bar 7's holdings. He turned over several schemes but none which could be figured to guarantee success. He was still working on it when a portion of the porch crowd began to drift away and, finishing his beer, Gill took a squint at the sun and told his reluctant helpers they could call it a day.

"No use to overdo it," he said, amused at the way Harry flung down his pick. "We'll get the rest in the cool of the mornin'. If you feel like a couple of drinks in the meantime just tell Quarls to put them on my chit."

He was about to move off when the Bar 7 boss caught hold of his arm. "You ain't goin' to have a heap of friends around here if your goddamn wire keeps our cows from that water!"

"*Friends,*" Gill said, smiling, "I wouldn't know how to deal with."

"What kinda guff is that?"

"Some," Gill said, unlatching Lockhart's grip, "might be shrewd enough to call it a word to the wise." And, leaving the scowling ramrod staring after him, he leisurely struck off in the direction of the feed lot where he'd left his team.

He found them munching contentedly on a bait of wild hay. Going back through the barn, he paused to hunt up the man in charge.

"Those two rannies," he said, "that came in last night with them posts have been engaged by me—"

"So I hear."

"Yes. Well, they're not what you might call real eager beavers. Occurs to me they might decide to pull out betwixt now and sunup."

"Shouldn't wonder."

Gill eased a ten spot between creasing fingers. "Be a favor to me if you could make sure they didn't."

"Take it up with Quarls. All I do is work here."

Despite these gruff words it was noticeable his glance didn't stray very far from Gill's kneaded bill.

"I expect," Gill said, laying it down beneath the lantern, "you could find some way of holding them boys over if you was to lay off and really put your mind to it." And with a wink and a grin, he set off to see what Quarls had for supper.

Which was a second thing about that girl he admired. She knew how to cook. She purely did.

In the bar, after eating, Gill treated himself to a pocketful of stogies and tried to work out in his head some surefire way of maneuvering Bar 7 into buying wire. While still neck deep in this he presently got to wondering about the credit situation with regard to Lockhart's outfit. Spewing smoke like a wood-burning engine on an uphill climb, he moved out of the bar to track down Quarls whom he found enthroned behind the store's counter soaking his feet in a pan of hot water. "Something ailing you?" he said.

"Nothin' I ain't put up with for forty years. What's gnawin' you now?"

"This Hallie Crockett," Gill said. "How big a spread has she got out there, anyhow?"

Quarls's eyes laid hold of him. "Big enough," he said finally clearing his throat. He mopped at the quiver of flesh beneath his jaws and tipped his head to study Gill's face through a couple more wheezes. "You could do a heap worse than hitch up to her."

Gill, grimacing, growled: "Not hunting advice, just a few plain facts. *How* big? Two-thirds the size of Rivas's?"

"Nearer, I'd say, on the downhill side of half."

"She got much influence with these two-bit outfits . . . ?"

"Who d'you reckon's goin' to listen to a woman?"

Ignoring the scoffing tone, Gill said, "If her daddy—"

"That was one thing. Hallie's somethin' else."

"Homelier, I reckon, than a Mexkin mud fence?"

"Don't know's I'd go that far. She ain't exactly lacked for suitors—could of been married couple dozen times over if Crockett hadn't kept that shotgun so handy. Said if he had to put up with in-laws, *he'd* do the pickin'." The storekeeper guffawed.

Quarls winked at Gill's scowl. "Be up for grabs now. She won't hev to write no heart an' hand column. You can put your money on that!"

Gill eyed the man with considerable distaste, then ironed out his face to say casually, "How's she fixed for cash?"

Quarls closed one eye and put a knuckle to his nose.

"What's that supposed to mean?"

"Maybe you better have a talk with Crockett's banker."

Gill studied it. "That's the best idea you've come up with.

Except I never knew one of that chintzy breed you could get much out of with anything less than TNT."

"Shouldn't be no problem fer a feller slick as you."

Gill sat a while squinting through a ring of blue smoke at the foxy lips above those shaved hog jowls. "Let's talk about Rivas. If this Crockett filly's such a plumb joyful armful, how come Rivas ain't chucked his hat out for her to dance around? Be a sight cheaper, looks like, than what he's layin' out to get roped into now."

"Who says he ain't?"

Quarls hitched himself forward to double both hands about the knob of his cane. His sepulchrally lowered voice held the slithery sound of a snake climbing out of its last year's skin. "Not many hereabouts cares to talk about him. But," he said, peering craftily around, "I'll say this much. Mostly it's account of her an' old Crockett he's made up his mind to shut off that water."

"Spite, eh?" Gill said.

With knuckle pressed to nose again, Quarls rolled his eyes. *"Pride!* Asked Crockett fer her hand, an' the old fool run him hell west an' crooked. You don't do that to a Rivas. Not in *these* parts! Crockett done worse. Told Mike, by Gawd, if he come suckin' round again, he'd cut off his prong with a hoof-shaper's nippers an' put it on public display in my bar."

"Lordy!" Gill sighed on an outrush of breath. But before he could pursue this gossip any further, the bespectacled Phil Sneed stepped through the front door with his arm round a bundle and his mouth popping open as his myopic stare discovered Gill's shape. It stopped him flat in his tracks like a caught fence crawler, the chagrin showing on him thick as cloves on a Christmas ham.

## VI

"What you got there?" Quarls asked, shifting gears to put a counter jumper's smile across those porcine features. "I'd give a leg pretty near to help you, Phil, but you know my views don't hold with barter. In God we trust. All others pay cash."

Sneed shot a flustered look in Gill's direction, eyed the fat man again, gripped his sack more fiercely in the clutch of both fists and with the gritted teeth look of an amateur conjurer dumped its contents on Quarls's counter.

Gill, amusedly expecting to see either a rabbit or a flock of soaring doves, glimpsed instead, through the wreath of fog from his stogie, a flap of bloody hide.

Quarls drew back with the sucked-in breath of an unwary pilgrim about to step on a snake as Sneed reached out to turn it hair side down.

"Pretty crude," Gill murmured, staring at the squiggles which had altered the original brand. "Feller did that must be a downright numbskull."

The Lazy S owner, with a snarl of indignation, cried, "Don't you believe it! Last week it was Cartell—this time *me!*" Shaking with frustrated fury he demanded of Quarls: "Can't you see what he's up to? We're being warned out! That Rivas crowd is setting this up to put on a full scale rustler hunt!"

Quarls dropped back in his chair, offering no comment beyond what could be read in the twitch of huge shoulders. But Gill said skeptically, "Why go to such bother if it's Rivas's intention to shut off your water? All he has to do is wait and—"

"Maybe he can't *afford* to wait! I'm no a damn fool! He's got some kind of deal on with Oleado's bank—Cartrell says they had their heads together over in Naco . . ."

Quarls's scoffing tone said, "How would he know that? Got him a Monkey Ward crystal ball, has he?"

"He saw them. Two weeks ago yesterday."

"What took that empty purse over the border?" the storekeeper asked with a lift of the lip.

Sneed reddened, fell a half step back to growl, affronted, "I don't stick my nose in other folks' business!"

"Well, bully for you," the fat man said, while Gill looked with interest from one to the other. "What are you figgerin' to do with that thing?"

The ranchman chewed at a cheek. "I don't know," he muttered finally.

"Then take my advice and go bury it pronto."

"What'll you take for it?" Gill asked, casually. And Sneed,

stiffening, said, "Why would you want to give anything for it?"

Quarls laughed with sour humor. "Huntin' grist for his mill. Ain't nothin' this new breed of drummers won't do to turn a quick buck—ain't you onto 'em yet?"

"Quit pullin' his leg." Gill sighed, sober faced. "Has it occurred to you, Sneed, packin' that round could get a man's neck stretched?"

The rancher peered at him grimly.

"What did you do with the carcass?" Quarls said.

"Had some of my neighbors in for a feed. What we didn't eat they took home with them, most of it."

"That was real bright." Quarls looked disgusted. "You're sure bent on playin' into his hands."

Gill said, "I'll give you ten dollars for that piece of hide."

Sneed's myopic stare rummaged him suspiciously. Then his mouth tightened up. "I guess not," he growled, stuffing it back in his sack. His glance swiveling to Quarls, Sneed said, "I think maybe Dugan could be interested in this."

"The brand inspector? Are you plumb daft? He'll go through hoops to stay on good terms with Rivas!"

"They've fell out," Sneed gruffed and, hoisting his sack, took his scowling departure.

In the shine of the lamps Gill could see Quarls's disgust. "Why don't he go to have a talk with the law?"

Quarls said with a sniff, "All he'd get outa that is a long ride fer nothin'—Cartrell found that out already. Sheriff sticks close to the county seat. Knows where his bread's buttered. Ain't enough votes at this end of the cactus to keep a dang gopher in grub fer a week." He swabbed at his chins. "I dunno about you, but I'm goin' to bed."

The next day Gill got the rest of his holes dug. But the following day when his roughnecks were due to start setting posts neither one of them appeared. Fuming and fretting he stewed around for another half hour before, with an oath, he took off for the livery.

"They've flown," Gramps said with an air of defiance. "I done my best but they took off anyhow. That big no good Harry stuck a gun in my ribs. Ten bucks ain't hardly worth gittin' kilt fer!"

The one thing Gill had completely overlooked was the thought of them departing without their wages. He said short tempered: "Saddle me a horse. And don't give me no kid's pony!"

Three hours later, abruptly cresting a ridge, he got his first look at Mike Rivas's headquarters and was considerably impressed.

Hacienda del Sol, built in the Spanish style of white-washed adobe, sprawled half-hidden beneath a grove of tall palms. It was a beautiful layout, as fine as he'd seen, and Gill sat a thoughtful five minutes admiring it. Sighing, he kneed the tired horse into motion. It looked the kind of spread he'd have liked for himself and, thinking about this, he sighed once again. Well, it wasn't beyond him, he grumbled, scowling.

The trail widened out, other trails slanting into it where cattle were in the habit of coming down from the hills. Along the dry washes they lay chewing their cuds in the shade of bean-hung mesquites and the yellow-balled huisache, whose perfume reminded him of nights left behind when, after the manner of wastrels, he'd squandered his commissions on whiskey and whores. But his wild oats were sown. He was through with that now, become a man to reckon with—the Number One drummer for Grudden's barbed wire!

Woodpeckers squawked from their holes in the saguaros, and on the dry, sun-scorched wind came a smell of growth and water and off yonder, behind the lush green of willows and cottonwoods, he caught occasional glimpses of the life-giving river.

He saw great fields of waving corn, rows of sugarcane, mangoes and the darker green of tamarinds and, against a sky that looked bluer here, the tufted tops of coco palms. The homemade tiles on Rivas's house sat blood red above the blue look of a long, deep gallery, comfortably furnished with hide-covered chairs to complement the earthen *ollas* and bright strings of pepper pods asway in the breeze under time-weathered rafters. Beyond the grilled window slots of thick plastered walls, he could make out the thatched huts of servants, the stables, a miscellany of corrals. The fellow lived like a king, Gill told himself sourly.

But he broke out a smile as a *mozo* appeared to stand by his knee while the *patrón* with cold eyes stepped off his verandah. Gill had heard no little of—even occasionally sampled—the old world courtesy of Spanish tradition, but found none of that here. Rivas, apparently, was a new breed of *rico* who cared little for custom and came to the point without waste of breath.

"What do you want?"

Well, Gill thought, that was blunt enough. But he'd come here prepared to get what he wanted and could very well manage without hugs and kisses. Chuckling, he said, "Figured maybe I'd show up in time for the feed bag, but you've already eaten—"

"If you've come for a handout you've got the wrong door. The *mayordomo's* quarters are off there by the stables."

"Ha ha!" Gill laughed. "Too shay, as the Frenchies say." Then, crooking a leg about the horn of his saddle, he looked the *hacendado* squarely in the eye. "Bein's you're hellbent, it seems, to get straight to business, I reckoned to drop by and do you a favor. Care for a smoke?" he said, holding out a stogie.

Rivas waved it away. It appeared he had heard of Greeks bearing gifts. "Either state your business or get the hell out of here."

"I want the loan of two men."

"You've got more brass than a damned gringo bedpost," Rivas growled through his frown.

But Gill only smiled. "Like they say, the squeaky wheel is the one that gets the grease."

"What do you want them for—and why should I put myself out for *you?*"

"Self-interest. I've run into labor trouble. Can't get no one to set them posts."

"No skin off my ass!" Rivas said with a snort.

"Better run that through the chute again. If that corral don't go up you got no deal, no free fence or anything else but a scrabble of nitwits all after your hide—maybe even a lawsuit if any of their cows turn up with lead in 'em."

Rivas's scowl grew more thoughtful, and Gill pressed his advantage. "Best way to make sure I don't pull no tricks is

to have that pen built by men you can trust. I'll even pay
'em day wages and feed them besides."

No one could argue with that kind of thinking. When
Gill set out for Quinn's Crossing half an hour later a pair
of Del Sol *vaqueros* rode in his wake.

## VII

BUT ALL IS NOT free that flitters, and Gill wasn't fooled into
imagining Rivas sufficiently naive as to leave to fickle chance
any more than he had to. With five hundred dollars, coin of
the realm, riding on every steer that broke loose—not to
mention the fence and services he'd been maneuvered into
buying if Gill's wire held them, you could pretty well figure
all bets would be hedged with private precaution passed on
to that pair behind the flat of his hand.

Gill was no careless dude or any part of a greenhorn at
grappling skulduggery or passing it out. He kept his weather
eye peeled and, while he didn't stand round with a hand on
his pistol, made it plain by his look that he could explode
into action without waiting for Congress to pass an enabl-
ing act.

It took two full days for the borrowed help to get the
posts set to Gill's satisfaction. Those Del Sol *vaqueros* weren't
the world's fastest workers but they were about the most
thorough of any *'paisanos* he had ever had truck with. With
beer mug in hand, he watched like a hawk as each post was
tamped, even attempting to shake each one as they left it
just to be on the safe side of judgment. Though filled with
increasing unease, he found in every instance not one thing
he could complain of. The posts could not have seemed
more solid had he personally set every goddamn one.

Yet Gill knew in his bones it did not stand to reason any
Latin Americans, of whatever persuasion, would so diligently
sweat to skin one of their own in aid of some *gringo* out-
lander. There had to be a hitch in this someplace, and all
through the heat of that second day he wore out his temper
vainly trying to lay hold of it.

In the end it was the girl, Quarls's Jude Jackson, the bareass bather, who put him on to what was up Rivas's sleeve.

He'd already hit the sack and was pounding his ear when a hand on his shoulder brought him bolt upright, fist clamped to pistol. When he made out who it was, Gill snarled at her angrily, "Ain't you got one damn lick of sense? Don't you know no better'n to wake a—"

"Shh!" she cried in a jumpy whisper. And, catching hold of his free hand, tugged him to the window, silently pointing.

The outside was so black he couldn't see anything to snarl at, till she said, with the breath warm against his neck, "Look at your corral!"

He still couldn't think what she was yapping about till the sliver of a moon, shaking loose of the cloud wrack, showed a vague blur of movement someplace back of those dark posts.

Not even bothering to pull on his boots, with gun still in hand, he went catfooting through the bar's heavy gloom to find the side door and ease it stealthily open. Standing there in his longjohns with the breeze off the peaks fanning back his tousled hair he could see considerably better, well enough to be sure somebody out there was fixing to cost him quite a pile of money.

The girl whispered nervously, "What do you reckon they're up to?"

"They didn't get up in the middle of the night to do me no favors, you can bet on that!" He said after some moments, "Wish to heck that moon was just a mite brighter."

He went back, fetched a chair and lowered his butt into it, keeping watch through the crack of that unlatched door; the girl, still back of him, breathing down his neck, a not altogether unpleasant situation though it did rather tend to be distracting.

After about twenty minutes of this, punctuated by occasional thumps and the labored sounds of panting grunts, whoever was out there packed up their duffle and slunk off through the shadows like a couple of wraiths. By this time, even with the light being poor, he'd a pretty good notion of what they'd been doing; but with her hand on his shoulder, and the clean woman smell of her calling up thoughts no right-minded man ought to be thinking, Gill sat on for perhaps a quarter hour remembering the look of her standing in that water down by the crossing.

With what may have passed for a gusty yawn he dumped the titillating notions back into his dream sack and got to his feet. "You know any way a feller could check if that pair of Del Sols is still in their soogans? I mean without putting them sonsaguns wise?" When she didn't at once answer: "They're in the stable most likely."

As she reached for his hand, Gill said impatiently, "It don't need the both of us. Just make sure they're over there."

"Where will you be?"

"I'm going to look at them posts."

He went back for his matches and got into his pants and, still in his sock feet, slipped out the side door. It didn't take long to make sure his hunch was right. You'd have thought at first glance not a post had been tampered with, but after shaking a few he got hold of one that was not as firm-seated as it had been when he'd left them. It was still pretty solid, but if enough of these posts had gotten the same treatment, the rough stock Rivas would be figuring to fetch wouldn't be hardly an hour getting free again.

Gill made a mark with his burnt-out match and started looking for others.

He couldn't afford to miss a dang one. It took him near half an hour to get round the lot and when this was done the count of loosened posts stood at twenty-three, four at one point, five at another, the rest of them spaced along the curve that flanked Quarls's porch where the store door was located.

He swore under his breath but was consoled by the thought that if he managed to get the weakened posts tightly set again without Rivas's pair catching onto the fact, there wasn't much likelihood they'd try something else. He was looking for the crowbar when Quarls's bound girl rejoined him.

"They're both in the stable snoring up a storm."

"You know what they did with that crowbar?"

Judith shook her head, but said when he scowled, "There's another in stock, but if you get it all dirty won't the cat be out of the bag?"

She was quick, that girl, besides being cute. "No," Gill grinned, "if it gets washed off and put back where it come from."

"Not sure I can lift it. It's a lot heavier than the one they've been using."

Following her inside Gill peered at the bar without much favor. No doubt about it doing the job, though he couldn't look forward with unalloyed relish to the prospect of spending what was left of the night with it. By sunup he'd be feeling like something pulled through a knothole.

It proved a pretty good prediction. The time was 4:15 by his hunting case watch when Gill, with every post set solid in caliche, finally dropped the scrubbed bar back into its slot behind Quarls's counter and groaned with relief. He hadn't felt so used up since his old man had belted him for taking that skunk into "Elder" Berry's Sunday School class and the old fool's daughter, with braces on her teeth, had been forced to bury every stitch she had on.

He may not have slept the sleep of the just, but the fat man was just sitting down to noon vittles with the girl waiting on him when Gill, bleary eyed and badly in need of a shave, stiffly got himself afoot to appear in the kitchen like a hung over drunk. Knuckling the side of his jaw through the rasp of stiff bristles, he wanted to know "where the hell them two hands" was, eyeing the empty plates beside Quarls's.

"Already stuffed to the nines an' hard at it."

"At what?" Gill said, blinking.

"Stretchin' wire. Ain't that what you're payin' them fer?"

Gill pawed his way across the room to a window. "I'll say this," Quarls grunted, "them two is real workers. Couldn't hardly wait, by Gawd, to git at it."

"Where'd they get the wagon?"

"Put it on your bill at the livery. Wisht I knew what you gingered 'em up with. If I thought they'd work fer me like that, I'd buy up their debt an' git 'em here permanent."

"Yeah," Gill muttered, coming back to the table. He stared at his food like the fish in his plate had been fried with the head on. All through the meal he sat wrapped in his scowl and Quarls, unable to drag a word out of him, finally got up in disgust and limped off.

"Ain't you going to drink that coffee?"

She had to ask him twice before the sense got through to

Gill, and even then, by his look it might as well have been ditch water. Putting down the cup he shoved back from the table, went off to find his pistol and stepped out across the porch without remembering to pull on his boots till Judith called the fact after him.

"What's stuck in *his* craw?" Quarls asked from the comfort of his seat behind the counter. But the girl shook her head and went off to tend chores.

Gill came back fully dressed, put his feet on the rail and tipped back a porch chair to keep an eye on progress, still with that cogitating look round his eyes. Only reason he could figure for that pair tying into the work like they had was they hadn't yet used up all their ingenuity. But he kept his mouth shut until the boys knocked off for supper.

"Tomorrow," he said as they stepped onto the porch, "we'll go over that wire and make sure it's not short stapled."

## VIII

OBSERVING THE WAY Ventoso's jaws came together—he did the bulk of their grumbling—Gill reckoned the nail had been hit on the head, and was sure of it when the stockier Vasco jumped in to say: "No need of that, *patrón!* We take care them steeples—git right on it soon's we're done eating."

"Fair enough," Gill grunted, hoping to sweep this under the rug, giving off with the quips and what he fancied was banter as they all pulled up chairs to the warmed-over fish and eel tails. Half a dozen times in the course of this chatter he found Ventoso's ungrinning scrutiny combing him over like a horse up at auction and too well knew he'd put his foot in it proper.

At the time, graveled and uncaring, it had seemed a good thing to loose a blast that came straight from the shoulder, letting them know he wasn't with impunity to be taken for a fool. A pretty stiff price to cough up for ego, the way he saw it now, if they went back and noticed he'd reset those posts.

In this foul mood, he growled at the storekeeper, "How far off is Bar 7 from here, Quarls?"

"You mean Crockett's headquarters? A six mile ride. Was

I in your boots I'd put it off till mornin'. That's a pretty
rough country to go rammin' round at night."

"Like to make sure they'll be on tap for this shindig."

"Try keepin' 'em away! Not a boy or his uncle will care
to miss that. They've all got a stake—"

"You sure we're oratin' about the same horse?"

"What other nag is there looks hotter'n this 'un?" The
fat man shook all his chins with a snort. "If any of that wire
goes round Middle Water you could turn out to be—hands
down—the best hated gent next to Rivas in this county."

"You can't have progress without a mite of pain—"

"Just keep that in mind while the clods is bein' tromped
down on your coffin."

Gill loosed a hoot. "I've heard the wind blow before." He
glanced around at a racket of chair legs to find Rivas's hands
on their way out the door. Stifling an impulse to trot along
after them, he said to the storekeeping boss of Quinn's Crossing, "Reckon that Crockett girl will be coming along with
'em?"

"If you're layin' off to get your cap set for her—"

"It's wire I got in mind, not matrimony," Gill said brusque-
ly, getting to his feet. He glanced up at Judith hovering back
of Quarls's bulk and scowled, turning red when she made
bold to say, "Better shear off them bristles if you're goin'
over there. That foreman of hers might get you mixed up for
one of them waddies that's been runnin' off their beef."

But she looked sober enough a quarter hour later when
she slipped out to catch him bound for the livery. "Better
take Quarls's advice and do your riding after sunup."

Gill said, exasperated: "What'd you do for passing time
before I come blundering onto your doorstep?" When she
drew back, eyes widening, he gruffed somewhat more civilly,
"I ain't about to get myself lost."

And felt the search of her stare. "It ain't only that." She
looked worried. "Lockhart's apt to shoot anything that moves.
You've picked a bad place to go. Del Sol's patrollin' that
stretch of the river and, what I hear, they're armed to the
teeth."

His mind still uncomfortably preoccupied with her, Gill
was turning under the livery stable lantern when the bark

of a pistol sent splinters flying from a wall board scarcely a hand's breadth from his head.

He dropped in a hurry, rolling through urine-soaked straw with a curse, to twist up breathing hard behind a thick stanchion, gun palmed and nothing to use it on. Peering hard at the hackberries bordering the lane, he was just in time to catch the hard-running sound of a horse going south through the flow of mealy shadows. Lockhart?

The hostler came frowning up into the light. "You again, is it? You got a real knack fer sterrin' up lather—first shootin' we've had here in two months of Sundays. Who was it?"

"Didn't leave me no card."

"Mean to say just shot—"

Gill thrust the six-shooter under his nose. "That smell like I fired it?"

Gramps shook his head but kept right on staring. "You musta seen somethin'."

"Well, I didn't," Gill said grumpily. "If I had he'd still be out there! Whereabouts does that Jingo jasper put up at?"

"Don't know nothin' about him," Gramps denied, moving off. "Don't know an' don't want to."

"I'd sure like his recipe for copin' with nosiness," Gill muttered, wheeling on a sudden inspiration to let those fence stringers know they were not dealing with any Johnny-come-lately.

He found Vasco pounding while Ventoso held the light. "That's right. One staple for each wire, every post," he told them. "Ten cents off your wages for every one that's missed." He disregarded Ventoso's sneer but when the stocky Vasco put a bracing leg back of one of the reset posts while he pounded, Gill's ragged temper flew straight off the handle.

"It ain't going to fall over, you hairy baboon! I've reset every one of 'em, an' if there's any more monkeying done on this job somebody ain't going to turn up for breakfast!"

Ventoso, face darkening, put down his lantern. "Do the rest yourself!—no *gringo chingao* kin talk to me like—"

Which was as far as he got before Gill's fist knocked his head half around, and Ventoso, off balance and back pedaling, went down in a jolting tangle of mixed arms and legs.

There was blood on his chin when he got his face up to find Gill standing over him. Ventoso dug a knife from his collar and Gill drove a boot hard against his jaw. While that foot was still off the ground, Vasco's thrown hammer knocked him into a sprawl.

But Gill saw the man coming and, when Vasco leaped to cave in his chest, was no longer there when the boots came down. Rolling, he caught the man's legs round the calves, upended and flung him crashing into a post. Vasco yelled but came up crouching, shirt torn, with a naked blade sticking out of his fist.

"Want to play rough, eh?" Gill grated, panting. When the man abruptly dived for him, coming in low, Gill sidestepped his rush at the last possible moment, grabbed the knife-wielding fist just back of the wrist and twisting, spinning about with the fellow, hiked Vasco over one shoulder and slammed him squealing into the wire.

He left his shirt hanging there and came onto his feet with a bloody back, both hands empty, fear and hatred in about equal parts glinting from the lantern-lit shine of black, half-shut eyes.

Gill waited while Ventoso, hanging onto his jaw, picked himself groggily up off the ground. "You want more you can have it," he growled through the rasp of lungs clawing for air. "What you got ain't goin' to be a patch to how you'll feel if I get any more shit over this pen. I want it finished and ready for your outfit's cattle by this time tomorrow. Now get the rest of that wire put up right!"

They were already working, sullen faced and contentious, when Gill put in an appearance next morning. But they gave him no lip and, as far as he could tell, hadn't given him cause for any further aggravation. Not that he'd have bet on this. Still belligerent, he went back in and ate the good sampling of bacon, eggs and hashed brown potatoes a subdued Jude Jackson set silently before him.

Washing this down with two cups of black java, Gill walked back to the job and with a no-nonsense stare made a round of the posts, testing each strand and every post it was nailed to. Then he fixed up a stogie, hunkered down in the shade, prepared to spend whatever time it might take to see the corral through to completion.

When the two Rivas hands started to knock off for lunch, he lifted the six-shooter off his thigh and said, waving them back, "You can eat when you've finished."

He got some pretty hard looks and showed a sour grin when they went back to work. After a while, the girl fetched him out some cold snacks and a mug of draft beer to help them slide down. "Just a minute," he grumbled as she was about to depart. He scrinched a look at the sky. "Occurs to me, if that rain holds off, you could be having some extra mouths to feed tonight."

"Friends of yours?"

"You might call 'em that. Tell old lard belly I'll be wanting accommodation for the boss of this outfit—"

She broke in to say, "I guess he'll want to know first if you've anything to pay him with."

"He kicking up a fuss about me?"

"He's fussing, all right, about that tab you've run up. I wouldn't try to leave, if I was you, without payin' it."

"Gracious! Mean to say Quarls doesn't trust me?"

"He's in business for cash, not promises. He's got a pretty big investment—"

"And a sight bigger markup!" Gill sourly told her, peeling off three twenties from a thick roll of bills. "Put that down as on account."

She asked, eyes widening, "Don't you want a receipt?"

"Don't worry about that. I've got all the receipt I need right here," Gill told her, confidently slapping the sag of his pistol. He handed his mug and tin plate to her.

"Where in the world did you get all that money?"

"Robbed a couple banks—ain't you got me pegged yet?"

She tucked the three bills into the top of her blouse, not appearing to know whether to swallow that or not. "Better have a care how you flash that around. There's some in these parts—" She broke off to stare. "What happened to them?"

Gill looked at his fence builders. "Got a mite careless."

"But that squatty one! His back's all blood—"

"He got into the wire. Bad stuff to fool with."

She peered at him dubiously. "Hadn't we ought to do somethin' for it?"

"He's tough. He'll live. If he's learned his lesson."

41

## IX

GILL, AFTER THE girl went into the store with his eating tools, got up off his hams to plop his butt in a chair and think. Among the subjects he considered was the piece of doctored hide the nearsighted Sneed had fetched over and finally gone off with. Could there be any truth in the man's conviction that the Del Sol boss was getting things ready to put on a rustler hunt?

Experience told him anything was possible where a rich and powerful outfit was hemmed in by a bunch of have-nots suspected of helping themselves to its beef. In a situation of that sort, most of the moguls Gill had rubbed up against would not be long in making up their minds to clean out what they'd regard as a rat's nest, the process often hastened by the added inducement of acquiring more range.

It could be that way here, and he sat a while exploring how best to take advantage of the tensions and hatreds any fool could see were building up; but who to prod and when to do it? Phil Sneed? Lockhart? That brand inspector, Dugan? And where did Jingo fit into this picture?

A hard nose of his sort was pretty generally a loner, but he could be working undercover for Rivas; Del Sol would not be the first Spanish outfit to employ a *gringo* trouble-shooter to iron out the problems other *gringos* made for it. Certainly the man looked rough enough.

But it was much more likely, Gill told himself, the fellow was one of those masterless drifters who, getting wind of a good thing, stand ready to move in and tear off with anything not nailed down. He might even be in on these cow stealing didos. Or pulling whatever strings came to hand to give the impression there were rustlers at work, increasing angers, stirring antagonisms in hope of a profit.

He *could* even be a deputy marshal, sent in to hold down whatever bonfires were thought to be smoldering.

Gill didn't put a heap of faith in Sneed's notion of Rivas and that Naco banker cooking up something to disenfranchise the small owner part of this community. But, still nudging Mike Rivas around through his thoughts, he saw once again in his mind the broad fields and lush greenery of Del Sol headquarters. If the source of this lushness were about to dry up, he'd an added incentive for closing off Middle Water from the hodgepodge of neighbors who had been making use of it.

Not that Gill cared anything for this beyond what use he could manage to milk out of it. He'd spoken straight from the heart when he'd told Quarls all he cared about was how many miles of his product he could unload on these folks in a hurry. Wire was his god, and he sold wherever a sufficient amount of money could be dug up to pay his commissions. And if the company got stung by some of the customers, the courts and their lawyers could take a lien on the property or sell the place.

He got up to take another squint at the sky, now more than half-hidden behind lowering black clouds. Lot of turmoil up there; and the close muggy heat daubing jaundiced tints on everything about him held promise of rain before nightfall. This, if it came, could be a real gullywasher, and thought of the wire he had ordered fetched in—a day late already—deepened his concern. Trapped out in those hills by falling rocks or dry washes turned into raging juggernauts, he could damn easy lose everything but his shirt. And Gill wasn't a man to take losses lightly.

He was standing there scowling when Jude Jackson came out with her arms full of dishes. She was off the porch, heading straight toward his bull pen, when the savory smells emanating from these jerked his head up.

"Where you think you're going with that?" he growled, jumping after her.

"Those boys haven't had one mouthful—"

"Yeah. Too bad about them! They can damn well wait till they've done what I hired 'em for."

Her mouth tightened. With a toss of her head, she started on again toward them; but Gill, with temper lost, made a grab, spun her round, cuffed the load from her hands—even looked about to slap an open palm against her face—till, getting hold of himself, he let his arms fall to his sides.

She said, with blazing eyes: "Go ahead and hit me!" Impatiently brushing a lock of hair from her nose, she added in a voice that bit with contempt, "Don't let these skirts cramp your style!"

Gill took it, red-necked, fists balled at his thighs, but the girl was too angry to leave it there. Womanlike she cried at him fiercely: "I expect you're used to pushing people around!"

What Gill might have said will never be known for Quarls picked that moment to waddle into the picture, all chins aquiver, a sawed-off Greener gripped in one fist. "What's the row?"

The girl said spitefully, "Look at that mess!" The dart of her hand was accusingly leveled at the scatter of food beside the overturned plates.

Both Del Sol *vaqueros* had quit work to watch, the shine of their stares caught and held by Quarls's gun. "I told her," Gill said, "they could eat when they finished. I've got a pen to build, man, and Rivas due in here tomorrow with them steers. By the look of that sky we'll have a storm bustin' loose—"

"Storm!" Judith cried. "It could go on for weeks lookin' a heap worse'n this an' never let go one damn drop of water!"

"Nevertheless he's payin' them. It's his right," Quarls decided.

"Don't they have any rights at *all?*"

"No concern of yours. You got plenty to do without stickin' your jaw into men's affairs," the storekeeper growled, coloring up himself. "Now git in there an' tend it."

The girl turned away like a wet-footed cat but, just before she went through the door, spun round with her eyes as big as fifty-cent pieces. "Must be a real joy in this world to be a man!"

Quarls's cheeks turned darker, but Gill suddenly laughed. "You got a real bobcat there," he said, chuckling. "Looks like you don't take her across your knee enough."

She was right, anyway, about the storm. It blew up a dust, showed some lightning and thunder, but no faintest sign of rain splashed down. Rivas's Mexicans finished the corral, and Gill, after having another look round, paid them off. Judith, fixing supper, gave each of them cheese and crackers to hold them over till the rest of it was ready.

Gill saw with curled lip how the pair, with their hats off, made bold to shine up to her—Vasco, especially, with his brown glittery stare taking in each swing of her blouse top as she beat up the batter. He couldn't see any sign that the girl even noticed. Probably didn't, he told himself, frowningly wondering why she wasn't in corsets, and if Quarls encouraged this for the increased contributions it fetched to his bar.

He went off in a huff to have a look at his horses, thinking folks ought to know their own places. Some parts of the country a man could get shot eyeballing a female the way those two were. If she'd been any kin of his . . . But she wasn't—and a damn good thing! Man had troubles enough without her kind dumped onto him!

Halfway to the livery, with the wind still kicking its way through the treetops, a sharper thought turned him around in his tracks.

He must be about ready for retirement to go off leaving that pair alone and unwatched while still within reach of a way to get back at him!

He broke into a run with the sweat laying cold on the back of his neck and a head full of things they might be doing to that pen. He doubted that much would tickle Mike Rivas more than finding he didn't have to go through with this.

But they were both on the porch sitting tipped back in chairs, while the wind whistled round them and the sky overhead turned steadily and swiftly more ominously black. Thunder cracked and banged through the canyons and against the dark cleft where the river dropped roaring to the rocks far below.

And then, with forked lightning lividly brightening the landscape, both Mexicans reared up to stand, staring and jabbering, as a mule's head and shoulders came swinging into view over the lip of the trail where it climbed from the ford to reach Quarls's store. And behind the first came another and another as Rivas's *vaqueros* peered in astonishment, until sixty of these animals had plodded into sight, grunting and groaning beneath the weight of huge packs.

Well up near the front rode a man dressed in leather,

high cheekboned, fiercely mustachioed and additionally weighted down with a surplus of pistols. Behind and afoot came a black Yaqui Indian and four muleteers—obviously fighters, all armed with rifles.

At the sight of these, Gill—with the fervor of a hostage unexpectedly reprieved—filled his lungs with new breath.

## X

AFTER THE MULES had all been unloaded, led away to the livery to be grained and watered, their packs stacked with care behind the Quinn's Crossing bar, the mustachioed man in his trail-grimed buckskins—before following Gill into the fat man's store—directed two of his rifle packers to keep sharpened eyes on the bull pen. None of this was lost on the Del Sol *vaqueros*.

"Quarls," Gill grinned, striding up to the counter, "this here's Mon Dieu, a fire-eating Frenchy from who laid the chunk! Give him the best room you've got—not to please me but on behalf of your health. Mon collects hair with the single-minded gusto some gents give to bounties, and he sure ain't particular whose hair he grabs."

"In that case," Quarls said with a fine note of irony, "it looks like you're goin' to have to let him have yours," and swung the book around. "Sign there," he told the Frenchman, putting out a pencil attached to a bit of string.

"My *hair?*" Gill stared.

"Your room—the President's Suite. None better this side of Tucson, an' there you'd pay eight times what I charge." Quarls looked at Mon Dieu. "You require iced water and a liveried valet?"

The Frenchman loosed a great guffaw and, leaning over the counter, bussed Quarls on both cheeks.

"Here, none o' that!" the storekeeper glowered; but Gill's fire-eating Frenchy exclaimed in delight: "A man, my God, what ain't afraid to spik hees mind!"

"More like," Gill grunted, peering down his nose, "he's taken that billing with a big dose of salt. Show him your parlor trick."

Out of thin air, it looked like, the Frenchman produced a handful of knives resembling miniature bowies which he tossed in the air one after the other and dexterously juggled for perhaps thirty seconds before, as though alive and diligently trained, each embedded its point with a thudding vibration in a neat, glittering oblong outlining the book he'd been asked to write his name in.

That Quarls was impressed nobody could doubt, with his eyes standing out like knots on a stick. He mopped at his chins and lumbered onto his feet gulping air with the wheeze of a leaky bellows. "Where'd you learn that?"

"Pouf—it ees nothing! Stand aside please m'sieu, w'ile I show you some theengs you tell children about." And, stepping back several feet to put the sharpened sides of the blades directed toward him, he whipped a short-barreled six-shooter from under his armpit and, with four reports crashing almost as one, sent as many knives whirling from the counter.

Catching sight of the stunned faces of his two erstwhile fence builders peering from the door: "Pick 'em up," Gill urged Quarls, "and if one of them stickers has so much as a dent you can chop off my nose and pickle it in brine."

Quarls, looking them over, showed the expression of a man who didn't believe his own eyes. "Sonofabitch!" he exclaimed, truly astounded, "must've clipped every one square on the cuttin' edge!"

The two Rivas *vaqueros* looked as though their eyes were about to roll off their cheekbones.

"You're losing your knack, Mon," Gill said disparagingly. "I can damn well remember when from that many shots you'd have knocked the whole lot flyin'."

"I don' trot like the colt these days, either. One grows old," the Frenchman growled in a tone of disgust. "Ask my wife."

Quick as a wink Gill cried: "Which one?" and Mon Dieu, through a grimace, laughed again.

Then he poked the spent shells from his six-shooter, thumbed in fresh loads and tucked the weapon back under his arm. Taking up Quarls's picketed pencil he signed the ledger, gathered his knives and chucked an inquiring glance at his boss.

Quarls, watching all this, asked, "You work for Gill?"

"Two . . . three year," the Frenchman said, straightening up to thump his chest like an ape. "Like hand an' glove," he declared, teeth flashing. "Closer even than these," he tacked on, with two fingers thrust under Quarl's nose.

"So that's where he gets all his gall," the storekeeper grumbled, and Mon Dieu threw back his head with a snort.

"Not that one! You know what he done once? Sol' fence to every mans in Bandera! Them bravos she take up collection —buy every stran' of wire in my packs. Make one stipulation: *Don' never come back!*" he said with a guffaw.

The hotel part of Quarls's establishment opened off a balcony over the bar and ran the whole length of that side of the building: seven rooms in all, two of these permanently occupied, one by the fat proprietor himself, the other by Judith. Two more were crammed with the accumulated clutter of twenty years of living at the top of this cliff.

Of the three remaining one was being used by Quarls's current barkeep and the largest was the one Gill had signed for, the so-called President's Suite, which he now moved out of to accommodate Mon Dieu, a piece of generosity he promptly regretted after one hard look at the only room left, a windowless cubbyhole about half the size of a traditional monk's cell.

Although left open to the rafters it felt, once the door was closed, not much different than crouching in an oven. He had been in jails more comfortable than this, and eyed the corn shuck mattress with its motheaten, old, blue cavalry blanket stretched across the rope-strung bunk with about as much enthusiasm as a man could fetch to garfish stew. But there was no use asking the Frenchman to take it; valued help was too hard to come by to risk hard feelings over anything so small as where a man slept.

Gill shoved his war-bag under the bunk, awakening a clatter as a graniteware chamber mug rolled back against the wall.

He went down to the bar and, fortified by a drink, pushed on through the batwings to ask Quarls sourly how much it was costing him to stay in that coop.

The fat man said, "Two dollars a night, but if it's too hot

fer you I got no rules says you can't bed down on the front porch if you've a mind to."

"I can do better'n that. You got a saw in this place?"

"What do you want a saw fer?"

"To cut a window."

"I dunno's I want that room disfigured." But, seeing Gill looking so determined, Quarls said, "There'll be a one dollar fee fer the loan of the saw an' five bucks more fer—"

"Chrissake!" Gill snarled, tearing off a five spot and clapping a cartwheel down on top of it. "You throwing the transportation in for *free?*" And, when Quarls began to roll up his eyes: "Gimme that saw, you highbindin' robber!"

It took Quarls a while to find a keyhole saw and, when he got back to the room armed with this, Gill couldn't locate a hole to start it in. Wet by now as though he'd come through a rain he opened up one with a blast from his shooter and pretty near sawed an entire wall from the room. After which, too stirred up to count much on sleep, he tramped the length of the trembling balcony to kick up a further racket pounding the door of the room he'd given up. But all this got from his French pack train boss was half a smothered grunt. Then the snores came again.

Gill swore with considerable fervor and went back to the bar to pour into the captive ears of the apron everything he figured was wrong with the world. A dozen tepid beers later he staggered up to bed, and the barkeep thankfully blew out the lamps.

The next day was the big one, and Quarls, to properly honor the occasion, unpacked and hung out a tattered Confederate flag from the porch roof. The town began to fill up pretty early, and to care for the rush he sent Judith in to back up the apron behind the mahogany, which, by ten in the morning, was packed six deep though the earliest arrivals, secure in good seats, stayed in their buckboards or the sweat-darkened leather of center-fire saddles.

Gill, red eyed and surly, stood with a brace of muleteers and the Frenchman by the Mormon hitch of the corral's open gate and peered at his watch at least twice each ten minutes till Mon Dieu told him irritably to "for Chrissake quit fidgetin'!"

Bets were being laid all around as to whether or not Rivas's steers would breach this newfangled contraption and, if they should, how many would do it. With the Frenchman taking on all he could get hold of, Dugan, the cross-eyed brand inspector, being elected to hold most of this money. If Gill took any fliers in this type of investment, it was not apparent. His whole mien was so querulous none but Mon Dieu even risked accosting him, though some in the crowd took this jumpiness for nerves and covertly increased the size of their wagers.

Not until the sun stood almost directly overhead with a lot of people grumbling did the Del Sol contingent arrive with Rivas's steers. The Quinn's Crossing mogul, dressed to the nines, rode point for his outfit on a black stallion heavily encrusted with silver. A true *reata largo* man, his *funda de pistola* was cut from the finest of leather, fringed at the sides as well as the bottoms, and the hand-braided quirt adangle from his wrist was the handsomest tool Gill had seen in a coon's age. A real *caballero*—no doubt about it. He even got a few cheers from those who figured him to come out the winner, though not from Phil Sneed or the ubiquitous Jingo, who stood with arms folded and a sneer on his lips.

Just prior to the advent of the star attraction—the bawling, raunchy, dust-raising brutes fetched to test Gill's wire, Reb Lockhart drove up with his boss in a buggy. She did not much resemble Gill's advance estimate based on the disparaging remarks made by Quarls.

Hallie Crockett, for one thing, was a heap better looking than he'd been led to surmise; older, too, though still indubitably this side of thirty, with hair like spun gold or a field of ripe wheat as it seemed to Gill, standing there peering across Mon Dieu's shoulder. He could see the thrust of her breasts even from this far and the way the wide mouth pulled away from her teeth as she put on a smile for those who called greetings.

He reached up a hand to sweat-dampened bristles and guessed somewhat sourly he could do with a shave.

It was then the crowd parted to make way for Rivas's steers being choused toward the gate by the rope-swinging racket of his yipping *vaqueros*.

## XI

WITH NO FURTHER TIME to indulge his fancies, Gill put Miss Crockett with other things stored for future attention and focused his stare on the boss of Del Sol, who apparently had impatiently been trying to catch his eye. "You ready for these brutes?"

"Turn 'em in," Gill called, and the *hacendado*, making a sign to his men, kneeded his black stallion past knots of gathered neighbors to where Gill lounged in the lee of the opened gate. Still frowning, the Spaniard asked without preliminary courtesies, "Where are those two fellows you borrowed the other day?"

"Right over there," Gill said, pointing storeward. Being fried in the trapped heat under the porch roof Vasco and the disgruntled looking Ventoso stood scowling with ill temper beside the black Yaqui.

Rivas lifted an arm in a beckoning gesture, but neither of them made any move beyond glancing uneasily at the Indian. "What's the matter with those fools?" the rancher demanded, and raised his voice in a shout. "Over here, *muchachos!*" He waved again, imperiously.

When neither man moved, Gill said casually, "Looks like that feller has the Injun sign on 'em. What'd you want them for?"

Rivas looked from Gill to the Yaqui and back again, jowls grimly tightened round the line of his mouth. There was an edge to his voice, and the neck skin above the top of his collar showed considerably darker than the bronze baked on it by his hours in the saddle. Scowling suspiciously across hooked beak, he demanded "That feller working for you?"

"Depends what you mean by work," Gill answered. "Whiskery Bill don't rightly *work* for nobody. Spends most his time doin' what comes natural: eatin', drinking, whoring around. The really big difference between his kind and pale-faces is Injuns, when they undertake to go through with something, don't let nothing stand in their way."

"And what would you say that one's doing now?"

Gill said, smiling up at him, "Seein' them boys of your'n stay hitched."

You couldn't get more blunt than that, but if Gill looked for Rivas to jump off the deep end, he must have been quite let down when the Spaniard, coldly eyeing him, mentioned, "I'm sure you must have irons in the fire you're counting on to show a larger profit than you can hope to get out of this. Let's fasten that gate and get on with it, shall we?"

"Suits me," Gill grunted, and waved to his mule men to put up the wires.

No sooner was this done when the crew which had fetched Rivas's steers to the shindig yanked off sombreros and, howling like Comanches, hurled them at the cattle which took off with tails up toward the pen's farther side, charging pell-mell straight for the strands of glittery wire between posts.

Staggered by the shock of impact, bellowing and snorting, they milled in confusion, till Rivas, snatching out his pistol, began firing over their heads. But all this accomplished, even aided by yells from his gesticulating crew, was to turn the crazed animals still more befuddled until Gill drawled sarcastically, "Let 'em cool off—you'll get no place that way."

Rivas shot him a look that would have withered an oak post but waved his men back. The hysterical steers, still snorting and bawling, went round and round trying to turn up a corner, something Gill in his experience had foreseen and countered by fashioning his pen after the manner of a bullring, completely circular.

When the steers finally quit to paw up more dust, he said over the clack of horns and grunts, "Ever watch a horse catcher sack out a bronc?"

The *hacendado*—far from a fool, regardless of temper—snapped this up straightaway and called out to Quarls to fetch him some blankets. "I'll get 'em for you," Gill offered, and did so.

With his crew charging and with the flap of these waving blankets, the cattle once again hurled themselves at the fence. Some of the confidence fell out of Gill's grin when a pair of posts snapped and, under the thundering massed weight of this onslaught, another leaned outward above the bulged ground.

But the frantic steers, thrown back on their haunches, took off through the racket to try a new spot. Time after time in their wild flight from the hecklers, they stormed other sections of Gill's thorny barrier without getting through.

After more than an hour of this kind of thing just about everyone but Rivas was convinced. The longhorns looked to have met their match. Groggy and heaving with each pant-missing breath, they appeared exhausted. Several had horns missing, two had broken legs and the rip of those barbs had put blood on all of them. Anyone but Rivas would have called it a day.

But the scowling Spaniard wasn't satisfied yet. Putting his horse through the crowd, he pulled up by Quarls. "You got a tarp or a wagon sheet handy?"

The fat man growled out a wheeze of protest. "An' who's gonna pay fer them goddamn blankets?"

"I'll pay for 'em," Gill grinned.

"Don't do me no favors!" snarled the rancher, affronted, and flung a fistful of coins at the storekeeper's feet.

"Pick those up, Jude, an' go fetch a tarp fer him."

"Too heavy for a girl," Gill pronounced, wheeling after her, unaccauntably flushing under Quarls's lifted stare.

When he came back with it over a shoulder, Rivas was instructing his perspiring *vaqueros* in what he wanted done with it. Gill tossed it down and the Mexicans, dismounting, packed it off a couple hundred yards and spread the thing out. They tugged it around till the nearest of the four corners faced the corral. One man ducked under the point, holding it over him, while two others caught up a corner to right and left of him. The remaining pair, armed with rifles, got under it, hiking the center part up with their gun barrels.

"Try it out," Rivas yelled; and the pair at the sides made their corners flap like wings. "Good enough," Rivas called, and fired off his pistol to get the cattle's attention.

To them, as it came charging down toward the fence, that tarp may have looked like some great wounded bird. Whatever it looked like it scared the hell out of them and—except for the pair of broken-legged steers—they all took off in a thunder of hooves toward the pen's farther side. But the broken posts dangling there turned them and, with the crowd scattering frantically, they went slamming into the side next to the store.

The uproar was monstrous from that terrible pile up, steers trampling steers in their mindless urge to get clear of this carnage—horrible enough to make Quarls puke.

But Grudden's wire held and Rivas, after that first stunned look, flung down his hat in a paroxysm of fury. Black as a thundercloud, he had his horse wheeled to ride off in a passion, when he found his way blocked. Mon Dieu had reached up to grip its cheekstrap.

Rivas flung back an arm, but the quirt in his fist was checked in mid-air when a voice at his stirrup softly drawled: *"Don't try it."*

## XII

WHETHER IT WAS what Rivas read in that frosty tone or the bore of Gill's pistol, so rigidly ready to blow half his head off, Rivas sat still as something hacked out of wood.

He finally drew a great breath and presently, carefully, let go the quirt before bringing his arm down.

The Frenchman chuckled, and there was a sizable jostle of men crowding round, as Gill, with his other hand, reached for an oblong of folded paper and shook it open for the rancher to look at. "This here is the agreement you made in Quarls's bar; confirms our conversation about the wire and services you engaged to buy in the event your steers couldn't—"

"I know what I agreed!" Rivas said, his face livid.

"Then put your John Henry on this. For the record. Those boys back in Chi is real sticklers for detail."

"What d'you expect me to write with?"

"Try this," answered Gill, and held up a pencil that, minus the string, looked considerably like the one Mr. Quarls had kept tied by his register.

Mouth tight, Rivas snatched it and, hoisting a knee, scrawled his name at the bottom and flung the thing back. Refolding and stuffing it into a pocket, Gill cheerfully told him, "Now you can make the down payment this calls for."

The rancher jerked up his chin, glaring down his long nose

like a bull just nailed with a full set of sticks. "Do you imagine," he grated, "I ride around like a bank!"

"I expect you must have a buck or two on you. Would these folks believe the great Mike Rivas could fetch himself to this gamble without a *centavo?*"

Rivas licked at the lips below his mustache while the stab of black eyes jumped around like a cricket. He said through clenched teeth, "How much do you want?"

"Well, enough anyway to cover expenses. Say . . . a couple of hundred?"

The Spaniard looked about ready to fly but could no more do it than he could afford, in front of this gawping multitude, to be held up to ridicule. With a smothered oath, he snatched out his purse and tossed it contemptuously into Gill's hands, glaring red-faced when the wire company's drummer ostentatiously emptied it into his hat and began quite clearly to count it aloud.

"Well," Gill said finally, quitting to peer up at him, "you're a few dollars short, but I guess this will do. Mon Dieu, write the man out a receipt for a hundred and eighty-two, seventy-five."

Rivas didn't wait for either purse or receipt but, quick as the Frenchman let go of his bridle, put spurs to his horse and hit out for Del Sol, his poker-faced crew pounding leather behind him.

"A great day for the Anglos," Gill told his Yaqui, and despite the hard losses his victory had cost them, those standing nearest sent up a thin cheer.

But Horatio Gill, despite what it did for his pocketbook and ego, was too experienced a hand to fondly imagine that his deflating of a man as important as Rivas would be permitted to end there. Any praise it had elicited from the have-nots would turn into curses, and, no doubt, critical abuse, when his wire kept their cattle away from that water. Nor was Del Sol's owner likely to forget what this employment of Gill was costing him, or the loss of face he'd so publicly suffered. Gill hadn't needed to rub the man's nose in it.

While in sober reflection he might wish he had handled the Spaniard more tactfully, Gill wasn't one to wail over spilt milk. Bright and early next morning he was en route with his mule packs, armed with reluctant directions, to search out Middle Water and set up his camp. Since this was no job to get through in one day, he had fortified his outfit with three extra pack horses, all heavily burdened with supplies from Quarls's shelves.

One of the chores bound to lengthen his stay was the problem of cutting and transporting posts, no way having yet been devised for hanging good Grudden wire on nothing more substantial than thin mountain air.

But there'd be other things, too, not the least of which could be diverse forms of harassment from the country's fenced out owners, who, sooner or later, would almost certainly get around to wire cutting. This prospect, of course, bothered Gill not a bit; the more wire they cut the more he could sell, when it got to the point where he couldn't find other ways. He had come prepared—in lieu of more customers—to spend the whole summer at Rivas's expense.

It was getting on toward dark when they came upon a ridge overlooking the broad basin where Del Sol, across the river, bordered the Crockett girl's Bar 7 holdings.

Save for one stand of trees, the view was barrenly empty, yet Gill found it extremely interesting, even though overgrazing during the current lack of rainfall had reduced the range to little better than a dust bowl. Still, the place showed definite possibilities when one saw what irrigation had done for the Mormon desert.

The biggest drawback to realization of such a dream was the high cost of surveying and leveling for ditches and laterals. Unless Hallie Crockett had been left better fixed than Gill had reason to think, the only one hereabouts with sufficient bank assets had to be Don Miguel, the Del Sol Minos.

Which could well be what the man had in mind. Cut off their water; starve them out; then buy up this basin for little or nothing. And Rivas looked foxy enough to embrace this scheme.

Bit of a gab with Miss Crockett might prove worth the time. There were several quick ways of putting wire on the market which seemed not to have occurred to most persons engaged in it.

Chuckling slyly, Grudden's Number One waved his mule handlers on and, beckoning the Frenchman, pointed out where they'd best set up their camp.

"Mon Dieu! On those *flats?* We'll be fried down to chitlins!"

"Thought I'd taught you better than that. They got a war brewin' here, case nobody's told you. Sleep in them trees if you've a mind to. When *I* bed down I don't want nothin' covering no approach to my nest."

"Bad place, too much bushes," the Yaqui grunted, eyeing the trees.

The Frenchman pawed at his cheeks. "Oh, well—*c'est la vie*. Two to one. The usual score. But if they can't get you there, anyone so foolish as to hunt your scalp won't have much trouble finding some other place to shoot from."

"Yeah," Gill sniffed, "I been learned about that," and told of his experience beneath the livery stable lantern.

"Who would do these theeng, eh?"

"Can't keep track of 'em," Gill said with a shrug. "Feller has to take *some* risks in this business. I personally figure to leap from the premise that every nut I deal with sooner or later's going to throw down on me. 'Jump first and talk later' my old man used to say when giving his version on how to stay healthy past a vigorous eighty."

"An' did he?"

Gill shook his head. "Came a time when the old gent didn't jump quick enough. Could happen to me . . . but a man shouldn't count on it," he grinned with a sardonic twist of the lips. "When I go down there'll be others with me, and don't you forget it!"

"Kill 'em all!" growled Whiskery Bill, jerking a finger across his throat. Without a hair on his face, the Yaqui was plainly misnamed but no one, eyeing him, could doubt his sincerity.

Mon Dieu, staring, gave an involuntary shiver and hastily moved conversation to a more restful subject; but now that he'd been reminded of life's chancy pitfalls, Gill pawed over in the back of his head who was most likely to have taken that shot at him. Vasco? Ventoso? The Bar 7 boss?

Not Rivas, certainly. The *hacendado* hadn't yet been in town—or *had* he? Because he couldn't think quite where to place the fellow Gill was inclined to put high on the list the uncommunicative, ever present, tobacco-chewing Jingo of the milky stare. That was one sonofabitch a man would do well to watch every second!

Gill was just sitting down to a late supper when a rumor of hoof sound jumped his hand from fork to the grip of his pistol. But the geezer who rode up out of the dark was no one he'd ever seen before. A typical puncher, to judge by his garb, with little to distinguish him from half a hundred others. The way he kept his horse turned, though this, of course, might not have been deliberate, any look at its brand was out of the question unless you got up and hiked clean around.

"I'm lookin' fer Gill."

"You've got the right camp. Go ahead, speak your piece."

"You're Gill?"

"That's right," Gill said, finger curved to the trigger of the gun in his lap.

"*Gracious* Gill?"

"You found more than one of us?" the drummer asked dryly.

The visitor, abruptly making up his mind, ran a tongue across lips to quietly say, "I'm from Bar 7—Crockett outfit. Miz Hallie said to tell you she'd like to have a talk with you before you start puttin' up that fence."

"She say where?"

"Bar 7, I reckon."

"She to home now?"

A nod was Gill's answer. "Well, you tell her," he said, "I'll try—but not promising—to get over there tomorrow."

## XIII

ONE THING GILL had learned in the course of his travels was always try, no matter the fracas, to keep the other gent a little off balance. This had to be one of his firmest maxims and had prompted the response he'd given Hallie's messenger.

There was nothing to show the man had come from Bar 7, but Grudden's Number One was much too cunning to exhibit his suspicions or limit his remarks to the letter of the truth. *Keep 'em guessing* was another little homily he liked and did his best to live up to. He'd no intention of going to Bar 7 or any other rendezvous proposed by other parties. Too many, now buried, had put their asses in a sling by confidently tripping into some cute spider's deadfall; which is not to say he wasn't sorely tempted.

Hallie Crockett had a lot of things going for her besides being the only other likely prospect for wire at this end of the cactus, and he'd been trying without much success up to now to figure some way of inducing an investment; but a man hunting profit did damn little business on someone else's terms. Gill still had a few trumps tucked up his sleeve which could always be pulled out of it if the time looked ripe.

He spat in the dirt as he thought over again the message that old-timer had dropped by to deliver. And the more he pushed the whole thing around the surer he became that whoever was behind this, it wasn't Hallie Crockett. "Must think, by grab, I'm soft in the head, tryin' a come-on transparent as that!"

It was a lead pipe cinch Rivas wasn't balmy enough to try such a dodge. Seemed more likely it had been instigated by the crackpot who'd tried to drygulch him at the livery. Some greasy sacker with two cows and a horse thinking to pass for a rancher. Any of that crowd could work up a sweat just brooding over the wire he was going to hang. Could even be that half-baked Sneed!

Picturing Sneed brought to mind again that bit of hide the fellow had fetched in to show Dutch Quarls. *That* just might be some of Rivas's doing if he *was* trying to frame a case against rustlers. Quarls hadn't appeared to put much stock in it, but in the storekeeping business he probably couldn't afford to. Still, he'd given old Short-Sight some pretty sound advice when he'd told Sneed to bury it.

Then Gill got to wondering if Lockhart had sent this horsebacker over. The Bar 7 ramrod wouldn't have had to bend his prejudice much to tie Gill and his wire right onto Rivas's wagon, and anyone in Lockhart's fix would be quick to count anything or any*body* likely to help Rivas a pretty direct threat to his own security and future. Given this much incentive the Bar 7 boss, with the kind of hate that he was packing, could well have decided to rid the range of so unwelcome an antagonist at first opportunity.

And then, of course, there was Jingo. No telling what that hard nose might be up to. Lockhart probably would be ruled by impulse, but Jingo looked the more dangerous of the two. He wouldn't waste his time beating round any bushes!

Yet, despite these risks, Gill did not appear likely to jump off the deep end or to be making preparations to dig for the tules. He leaned toward the notion that what would be was going to come along regardless. Worrying about it wouldn't butter many parsnips. If a man kept his wits about him and a pistol oiled and loaded, he stood a fair to middling chance of being left alone.

On this theory he climbed into his blankets not even bothering to pull off his boots.

The alarm clock he'd set in his head before retiring got him up and about well in advance of the sun's first shafts. After a hard look around, he poked awake the sleeping mule man that was handiest. "You'll cook today," Gill said. "Get up an' start throwing something together."

With a handful of pebbles he then moved off to tease the snoring Frenchman out of his blankets. Mon Dieu, perhaps dreaming himself the target of some persistent botfly, slapped increasingly more fiercely wherever Gill's pebbles struck him until, cuffing his nose with enraged irritation, he jumped to his feet to owlishly glare at the chuckling joker hunkered just out of reach. "Sonomabitch! Some time, by gar, you catch knife in de t'roat! W'at you want wake me up middle of the night for?"

"Time's awasting. We got a fence to build."

Mon Dieu told him bluntly what to do with his fence, and Gill went off laughing to get the rest of them up.

But the wrangler, when he set off to fetch in the mules, came back angrily swearing. "Some swivel-eyed polecat's run the whole bunch off!" he lividly told Gill, slamming down his hat. "Ain't a one of them in sight!"

They had to spend half the morning rounding them up, by which time Gill was in a foul mood himself. "Leave someone around to watch the wire and these heehaws," he growled at Mon Dieu, "and take the rest of these loafers and rustle up some posts."

"Where you t'ink I find posts, hah?"

Gill waved an irascible hand at the mountains and strode off to saddle up one of his team.

It was close on to two by the look of his shadow when he reined the horse in before the deep gallery at Rivas's headquarters. He changed his mind about getting down when a *mozo,* meanly eyeing him across a lifted rifle, tossed out a gruff, *"Hola! Qué pasó?"*

"With your permission," Gill said, "I'll take that up with tthe *patrón.*"

Rivas poked his head out the door. "Get on with it then."

It was plain there wasn't any friendliness in him and not much patience if judged by his tone.

"Somebody ran off my mules last night."

"If you imagine I've nothing better to do—"

"Ain't suggesting you did it. What I want's enough help to—"

"You'll get no help here."

Gill took time out to consider him carefully. "Wouldn't think you're the sort who'd relish watchin' good money get poured down a rat hole; your money, at that. Maybe you better put some thought on this, mister."

"Don't come crying to me with your troubles."

"In the end it's like to be *your* trouble, Rivas. We got a contract—remember? All I've engaged to be responsible for is fencin' off that water. Maybe you don't give a goddamn, but if these two-bit bastards can run off my mules they can damn well just as sure cut your wire. And a heap faster, probably, than I can put it up."

Giving this time enough to soak through the poncho of Rivas's resentment, Gill wheeled his mount again toward the gate. The rancher growled: "Hold on!" And Gill, stopping the horse, looked back across a shoulder. "Yeah?"

It went sore against the *hacendado's* bruised pride to have any traffic at all with this *gringo* who had already twice, before his compatriots, pushed at him a plate of crow to wolf down. Yet it was obvious the man hated almost as much to be paying for something, which, if Gill was proved right, he'd not be allowed to get any use from. After clearing his throat, and swallowing a time or two, he reluctantly asked how much help Gill would need.

"They're your neighbors, Rivas. Don't short hand yourself. It's *your* wire they'll be cuttin' once I've got the stuff up."

In the end Rivas grudgingly mounted four hands, two of these being Vasco and Ventoso, neither of whom appeared overjoyed until the *patrón* said Vasco was to be in charge of the expedition. At this good news the gangling *vaquero* showed his teeth with great relish. "Si, Don Miguel. I shall be most diligent looking after your interests," he declared, slyly peering at Gill from beneath his huge hat brim.

"You bet," Gill assured them. "When that one gets through flinging bullets around you can probably file claim on a lead mine around there"; and then he rode off.

It was late afternoon with the sun a red ball that appeared scarcely inches above the dark spine of the westerly peaks, when Gill and his *cuadrilla* arrived at the camp to find the black Yaqui groggily nursing a near empty bottle. Knocking it out of his hands in a temper, Gill cried, "Where the hell are them mules?"

Ventoso loosed a malicious snicker when Whiskery Bill, peering stupidly about, instead of answering scrabbled after his bottle. Not a solitary mule loomed anywhere in sight. Under Gill's furious stare Vasco, reckoning he'd better lend a hand, ordered the Del Sol contingent into the field. Gill, taking time to make sure of the wire, kicked his horse after them, ragefully swearing. If this was the pattern he would have to string fence by, he could be here all summer and well into the fall!

## XIV

As GILL HAD more than half suspected, the mules had simply been driven off and scattered; none had been stolen. And if that didn't point to two-bit neighbors, led or instigated by Reb Lockhart, Gill stood ready to eat every one of them: hats, hide and boots.

Fortunately, the job of rounding up the animals, with everybody mounted, took a lot less time than it had after that first raid. Even so, it was well on toward ten before they finally got them all back into camp, securely picketed and put under guard. And it was then that Gill became uneasily aware that the post-chopping detail under Mon Dieu should have been back a good while ago.

By midnight, still with no word or sign of them, worry had the scratch of its claws deep into him. He was mightily tempted to tear off and hunt; but he was pretty damn sure Rivas's hands wouldn't join him, and prowling around in the dark by himself might be just what they hoped if the Frenchman's party had got into a bind engineered by persons opposed to what he'd come out here to do.

He eventually pulled off boots to wrap himself up in his blankets, but not much sleep came his way. Getting up red eyed to wolf down the grub flung together by one of the hands from Del Sol, he looked mean enough to skin the first man that got in his way.

Whiskery Bill, hung over from the bottle some fool had given him, was surly as a goddamn centipede with chilblains; nor was Vasco notably improved by the prospect of spending his time during the heat of this day chasing round through the hills on a hunt for people his whole outfit resented. But Gill's biggest headache stemmed from how many hands he dared take out of camp. He didn't crave any more saddle pounding on behalf of those mules!

In the end he conceded this was his responsibility and set off to find his post choppers without any help from Rivas's *vaqueros*. Though none of them offered any comment, it was obvious Vasco was considerably astonished that he would venture forth alone.

Pointing his mount toward the nearest line of mountains, Gill rode steadily through the early morning hours. When the sun began to really bear down, the foothills wobbling through their film of heat didn't look to be more than three or four miles away yet it was close onto noon before he got into them and began casting round in the hope of finding tracks.

Cow sign was plentiful on this barren range, but what few horse tracks he uncovered were days old and mostly left by unshod broom-tails. The few cows encountered stood droop headed on braced legs, unmoved by his presence, too listless even to get out of his way. Neither feed nor water was hereabouts apparent and, by their apathetic look, it seemed likely these critters would go on standing there until death put an end to their misery.

It was a hard thing to look at, but Gill's mind was on matters more important to him, like the futility of pushing deeper into the climb of hills farther up when he hadn't one damn thing to go on. This had seemed, back at camp, the nearest approach to timber, but if Mon Dieu and his crew had come this way, he hadn't found any sign of it.

Mon Dieu, in Gill's experience, was not one to shilly-shally round about anything. He was a simple man, used to solving his problems in direct fashion. It seemed logical to assume he'd set forth much as Gill had, aiming for the same blue crags Gill was peering at. He could easily have passed within a few hundred yards of where Gill sat in the sweaty cramp of soggy leather. The thorny nub was which way to turn to come onto his tracks—left or right?

Gill saw only one way to find out and that was to look; so, irritably growling as he pawed at damp bristles, Gill kneed his sweating horse off to the left.

But after a twenty minute ride without avail in that direction, he wheeled the reluctant horse about and pointed him east to get down from the hills and back on the flats, hoping to rectify the mistake of not starting his hunt where tracks would show plainly and the terrain could be covered in much less time.

It was almost two o'clock when he finally picked up the sign he was hunting, and then to his astonishment the tracks he sat eyeing, mule sign mostly, all were pointed arrow straight toward camp!

Not until he'd climbed out of the saddle was he reasonably sure just how fresh this sign was. Even then, it wasn't until he saw the barred mark left by the right hind hoof of Mon Dieu's horse that Gill was able to pour out a few of his most cherished cuss words. *All that worry and hunting for nothing!* Gill's relief was displaced straightaway by an anger so fierce that no sooner did he get his rump back into leather than he booted his mount toward camp at a gallop.

And there, sure enough, he found both the Frenchman and all of his crew.

The whole caboodle were just sitting down to fill up their bellies when Gill came storming into the camp. "Where the hell you been all this time?" he yelled, pinning the astonished Mon Dieu with his glare.

"Where the hell you t'ink? My God, I go where you tell me, looking for posts!"

"Damn if I see any!"

"We did not, either."

"You expect to find 'em all piled up an' waiting?"

The Frenchman, bristling like a dog with a bone, cried: "Me, I am not your peon—remembair? Tomorrow we look someplace else. Or maybe you like to go find them yourself?"

Gill said more reasonably, "Why couldn't you latch onto any?"

"I am not Jesus Christ! A man does not get blood from the turnip. Nor cut friggen posts where there aren't any trees."

Gill pawed briskly cheeks. "No trees at all?"

"Some catclaw. Some yucca. About so high," the Frenchman declared, flattening a hand by his belt. "You like posts from them?"

Gill stared back at the mountain his crew had just come from. "All right," he said with his glance swiveling east. "Any post oaks or piñons or juniper over there?" he called out to Vasco."

The Del Sol straw boss took a look where Gill pointed. "No, *señor*. Mesquite and greasewood. Plenty pear over there."

"What's the matter with cuttin' our posts from mesquite?"

The Mexican shrugged. "As you please, *señor*."

"Yeah. Well, it'll please me considerable if you'll take Mon Dieu and his boys there tomorrow," Gill said with a look that brooked no further nonsense. "We got a job to do here and the sooner it's done the quicker I'll be on my way someplace else."

Scraping the wiry growth off bronzed cheeks, Gill went on with ablutions, ignoring the sneers these attentions were getting from the Rivas contingent. According to the way his pappy had raised him, any gent who took no pride in his looks had to be either dead, past eighty or plain no-damn-good, and Gill didn't count himself in any of these categories.

Leaving Ventoso with the other pair of Del Sol hands to keep an eye on the wire and what mules Vasco and Mon Dieu had not gone off with to fetch back the posts, he threw his hull on one of the wagon horses and went loping off to see how the weather was over at Bar 7. Not that he conceded any great amount of credence to the message the Crockett girl was alleged to have sent, but he wanted to see if he could get any line on what that long-legged Lockhart was up to.

The morning was half gone when, from the top of a bluff, he got his first look at the Crockett headquarters. A typical layout for that time and place. A 'dobe bunkhouse, a huge paintless barn of whipsawed pine with the left over odds and ends from its building frugally used to piece together the weather-warped house that took Gill back to the sharecropper shacks along the Texas-Arkansas border. No *gringo* cowman he had bumped into yet could find any sense wasting money on "fixings" that could better be used to buy stock and care for it. In his experience they were all alike: bullheaded and contrary as drunk squaws.

But his brows pulled down in a long hard stare when he caught a good look at the jigger holding down the railless front stoop. With his back to a post and a Winchester rifle across the bony knobs of knees wide spread in the rust-colored sailcloth of "Texas" pants, there could be little doubt but that this was the same saddle bum who'd ridden into his camp with the invitation.

So maybe it *had* been from Hallie at that. Maybe it had not been just a ruse to set him up for some team of drygulchers. Perhaps he had better keep an open mind till he heard what the girl had to say for herself.

He rode on, came into the yard with a nod while the guy with the rifle stared mockingly back. "You the new boss?" Gill hailed with a grin. "What happened to Lockhart; he die of a stroke?"

"Had to ride into town."

"What's the smokepole for? You figurin' to stand off Geronimo's Apaches?"

"Apaches or Mexkins, they're all one to me."

Gill, narrowing his eyes, said, "Miz' Hallie to home?"

The screen door screaked as her hand pushed it open. Miss Crockett said, "Do come in, won't you?"

Gill, touching hat, got out of the saddle. "All right if I tie him to one of these posts? He ain't broke to ground like these cowpuncher horses."

"Hank'll watch him for you." The woman stood aside to allow Gill passage, hastily pulling the door to behind him. "These flies!" she said, wrinkling her nose. "You'd think by this time, I guess, I'd be used to them. it down, won't you?" she said with a smile, and watched Gill perch gingerly on the edge of a sofa. Settling herself in a hide-covered chair, she asked, without any further preliminaries: "Have you started putting up that fence yet for Rivas?"

Gill shook his head. "Waiting on posts."

"What would you say if I offered to supply them?"

When he saw she was serious Gill said, staring, "I'd say it's about the last thing I would look for, things bein' like they are and—"

"I'll be happy to get out your posts," she declared, "if you'll put up that wire for me instead of Rivas."

He may have been mistaken about what he thought he saw in those pansy eyes, but there wasn't one thing wrong with Gill's hearing, and what she'd just said was so totally unexpected he had to gulp twice to catch the real meat of it. "Y-you mean," he growled, floundering, "you mean . . . ?" and tried again to get over the turn this had give him. "You honestly expect me to sell a galoot of that caliber short?"

"For a consideration, yes," she said, again wrinkling her nose as a shift of her posture permitted a brief glimpse of a length of pink limb seldom seen anywhere outside a straddle house.

Gill caught his breath, truly shocked by this overture, but no longer doubting what he'd read in her stare. Cheeks flushing hotly, he got to his feet to back off a few steps; but no amount of embarrassment could sweep from his mind the rock hard foundation every deal must be built on. "The prime consideration I have to look out for is whether you got the money to pay for it."

"I think I could get it by the time it comes due."

" 'Fraid that's not good enough." He snatched up his hat in a sweat and got out of there.

## XV

WELL, GILL REFLECTED, scowling at Hank as he stepped from the stoop, the world here of late was plumb full of surprises. Still, he had to admit as he swung into leather, short-handed and desperate, in the kind of bind *she* was in, a feller couldn't blame her for trying.

Getting down again, ignoring the rifleman's lifted smirk, he went back to the door and, pounding upon it, said to the woman when she got up to look out at him, "Tell you what I *will* do, ma'am. I'll pay five cents a post for every one your hands chop out for me. This way my own crew—"

"Do I look hard enough up I would cut my own throat by giving you comfort in that sort of fashion? You know what that fence will do to this outfit!"

"Well," Gill grinned, "you could always cut it," and watched the hard slant of her stare turn astonished.

Dubiously regarding him, she chewed at her lip, then asked in a tone stretched thin with suspicion, "Why would you put such a thing in my head?"

Gill said, perfectly sober, "I'm a wire drummer, ma'am; make my livin' from supply and demand. Don't make me no difference what happens to the stuff once I've got it up," he enlarged, chuckling and nodding when he saw how quick she was to take hold of that. With a broad wink he said, "If you *do* decide to try out your pliers on it don't just leave the stuff layin' there. Rip out a good piece and snarl it up proper."

"When would you want those posts?" she asked, staring.

"Sooner the better. An' fetch plenty of 'em."

For a half hour or so on the way back to camp Gill rode in a euphoria of self-congratulatory satisfaction. It wasn't every day a man could turn up a piece of business as providential as this. With Bar 7 hustling posts for him and passing on his tip to diverse greasy sackers, he stood to make a good thing out of Rivas. And with his own crew freed to set the posts and put up the wire, from where Gill sat things were looking pretty rosy if everything went according to plan.

He guessed it was time to fetch Rivas over and show him just where he should put his fence. And not to waste any time, he took a squint at his shadow and forthwith turned his mount toward Del Sol.

Cutting diagonally across the range, he was able to reach the Spaniard's headquarters a great deal sooner than would have been the case had he first returned to camp. He had no illusions about Rivas feeding him, but Gill was a man who'd forego a meal any time if by so doing he saw the least likelihood of turning a profit. Thus he came into the Del Sol yard in the early middle of what traditionally in this part of the country was regarded as "siesta"—a time to rest tired muscles and recuperate the soul.

There being no one in sight, Gill sent up a hail. When this failed to elicit response he got down with a scowl and was crossing the gallery, bound for the door, when a *mestizo* in cotton *pantalóns* and crossed bandoleers stuck his head round the corner, pulling up in midstride to query sharply: "*Quien es?*" above the shine of a smokepole, which swung to bleak focus.

It must have seemed to Gill, in his apparent irritation, that every place he went anymore some hard nose was standing around with a rifle. "Looks like you'd know me by this time," he sniffed. "Where's the boss?"

"He sees no one."

"Not prayin' for rain, is he?"

When the man looked confused: "Just tell him I'm here," Gill said with a snort.

"For why, *señor?*"

"Because, by God, I said so!"

"Do all *gringos* jump when you open your mouth?"

"Somebody's got to say where to put thaat fence!"

"Around the water, of course."

This fellow was sharper than a five dollar razor. Nettled,

Gill began, "A guy with a mouth big as yours—" but broke off at the sound of spur-weighted boots.

"You again!" Rivas gruffed from the door. "What is it this time?"

"If you don't mind the ride, I'd be obliged if you'd show me just where you want that piece of fence put."

"Couldn't it wait till tomorrow?"

"Puttin' off till tomorrow somethin' ought to been took care of yesterday is how come you fellers lost this country. You want I should use my own judgment about this?"

"Pablito," Rivas said, "get a horse for me. *Pronto.*"

Gill had thought that would fetch him; but the rancher wasn't one to hobnob with hired help, especially a *gringo* so diligent at making himself obnoxious. Rivas made the whole trip in frozen-faced silence.

The afternoon's shank was pretty well shot when they rode into Gill's camp a mile west of the river to find the Del Sol cowboys, Ventoso included, hunched over a saddle blanket gambling with agates in lieu of hard currency.

Ventoso sprang up in considerable haste when he felt the cold stare Rivas clamped onto him. "So this," said the Spaniard, "is the measure of your regard for my interests. I put you in a position of trust and this is how you repay my confidence?"

The man looked like he'd been caught with his pants down. Twisting the hat in his hands, groveling eyes jumping round like crickets, Ventoso squirmed. "A thousand pardons, *patrón,* but it was not I who was put in charge. You told Vasco—"

The glint of Rivas's stare turned sharper as it quartered the view. "And where *is* Vasco?" he inquired, butter soft.

Ventoso's eyes jumped to Gill, who said, "He went off with my crew to find posts for the fence. If you'll show me now whereabouts you want it . . ."

The rancher dug a heel in his horse and rode toward the river, Gill following, thoughtfully turning over in his mind how best to use the hold Rivas's anger had so gratuitously handed him. If he couldn't make Ventoso and Vasco toe the mark now, he had damn well better swap his wits for a plow.

When they reached the water, the *hacendado* hauled his

mount to a stop and waved a hand up and down the bank. "Put the fence here," he said like a king.

And Gill said, "Sure. But how far north and how far the other way?"

"Two miles."

"Each way?"

Rivas peered at him sharply. "The idea," he spoke finally as though to a moron, "is to keep other brands away, is it not?"

"Well, sure. But they're away from it now."

"Because my *vaqueros* have chased them away. But they can't spend all their time turning back stock."

"In that case, what's to prevent Bar 7 cows, for instance, from following the fence to the place where it quits and—"

"Two miles south the river goes underground. Two miles north it flows through a jungle of lava rock too rough for cattle."

"Okay," Gill said, "but where it goes underground they've only to round your wire to get at it. You thought about that?"

Rivas curled back his lip. "Cows would not follow a fence that far. They've neither the brains nor the patience."

Gill said with a shrug, "Expect you savvy cows better than me. But if they do get around after I'm gone, you're right back to shooting 'em, an' once you start that you could wind up in court paying three times in damages what another couple miles of fence would of cost you."

"And who do you think would take me to court?" Rivas sneered, looking down his long nose at Gill. "Bar 7?" He laughed. "Your *gringo* police will not come—"

"There are federal police. We call 'em *deputy marshals.*"

"I spit on them!"

"You start shooting cattle you may have the chance a heap sooner than you think," Gill told him wryly. "What do you reckon that Jingo's hangin' round for?"

Rivas looked at him carefully. "That shit is a *marshal?*"

"Alls I know is him and that Bar 7 boss seem to be finding a powerful lot to talk about. You reckon he's tryin' to get a job with that outfit?"

Rivas tugged his mustache, looking angry and suspicious. But concern showed, too, as he pushed this around. He said at last with a scowl, "How much extra fence would be enough do you think?"

"Another five miles ought to keep them steers out."

"Nine miles of fence! Do you think I am Croesus?"

"Better sure than sorry," said Gill sententiously. "You could fare a lot worse if you get into court."


## XVI

AFTER RIVAS took off, having reluctantly agreed to three miles of extra fence, Gill, in the glow of this latest accomplishment, struck out for camp, getting back to the wagon to discover the guards dozing under tipped hats. He came in on the run, yipping like a mule eater, laughing uproariously when Ventoso and the other two, scrabbling madly for rifles, jumped to their feet, wild eyed, as badly shaken as though expecting any moment to see the last of their hair.

Ventoso put a sour grin on his whisker-stubbled face, doubly chagrined to be caught out by this pig of a *gringo*, who not two hours ago had seen him quaking under the wrath of his angry *patrón*. Having no ready excuse, he tried gruffly to cover this present dereliction by laying it to being up all night watching over the mules.

"Yeah," Gill nodded. "A hard life, ain't it? But cheer up, *amigo*. Tonight you shall sleep like a *rico*. From here on out all you've got to do is cook for this outfit."

"But, *señor*," the man cried, "I am no cook!"

Gill flipped him a grin. "Not to worry," he said. "You will be before I get done with you."

He got out of the saddle to find the other pair gawping. "Boy," he growled, catching hold of the nearest, "take care of this horse. And you," he advised, tapping the other with rigid forefinger, "get a fire started and start rustlin' supper. *Pronto!*"

He put his back to a rock, resting tired muscles while he watched lifted dust lazily drift toward the camp. Mon Dieu and his post cutters, he guessed.

And was right. It did his heart good to see the burden

being packed into camp by the twenty stout mules. Leaving the rest to unload he beckoned the Frenchman aside.

"Tomorrow we're startin' work on this fence. We'll be stringing seven miles of it, four this side of the river. Better divide your crew into shifts, biggest half of 'em digging." He explained the deal he had made with the Crockett woman, and the Frenchman whistled.

Then he pulled off his hat. "By gar, I don't know . . . You t'ink they'll deliver?"

"Five cents a post kind of argues they will; anything'll please Lockhart if it aggravates Rivas. Besides," Gill said, "tearin' up fence always tickles the have-nots. These squatters round here oughta have 'em a field day once we start puttin' up that wire."

Mon Dieu grinned. "For every rod they pull down we sell another!"

"Ought to work that way for a while, anyhow. We better try and get out before the guns start to bangin'. Push the boys all you can. I've fed him a line about that guy Jingo, but he won't take being whipsawed for long."

"He's got a pretty short fuse," Mon Dieu nodded, and went off to hustle the work of unloading and make sure each mule got a ration of oats.

A good while before sunup, to be more precise, about twenty after three, Gill rousted Ventoso out of his blankets and built up the fire. "Sling on the grub, an' don't be all day at it. I want those posts at the river and my crew along with 'em by the time it gets light enough to see what we're doing."

Then he got up Vasco, who had taken first watch, and told him to call in the others for grub. "We're going to move camp, bring it nearer the job; you tell your boys to give Ventoso a hand. My Yaqui'll take care of any mules we ain't usin'," he told Vasco's scowl.

The man stared and spat. "We are not your servants to order about. The *patrón*—"

"Your *patrón*," Gill said grimly, "is paying this outfit to put up fence. Anything hinderin' costs him hard cash. You want me to tell him you're too good to help get this job finished?"

When the man went off muttering, Gill got the rest up. By five o'clock, fed and mounted, the whole entourage, mules, wire and posts, weren't over a stone's throw from the damp mucky smell of the silt-clouded river. "Set the camp up right here," he ordered Ventoso, peering round through the dark from the rise he had stopped on. Already flecks of pink were beginning to be discernible off to the east.

He turned to Mon Dieu. "I'll drive the team down to the river, and one of your boys can drop off these spools at suitable intervals; tell them others to do the same with the posts. That way we'll have 'em reasonably near where we're working. Vasco's *vaqueros* can keep a watch on things for us."

One of the Frenchman's Mexican mule handlers climbed up beside Gill at a word from Mon Dieu, and Gill clucked to his team and drove off to get started.

They worked straight through the day not even stopping for grub, until it got too dark to pound any more staples. When they finally knocked off, better than a mile of new fence stood behind them, and all but the Del Sol contingent rolled into their blankets as soon as they'd eaten.

When Gill piled out of his soogan next morning, he was pleasantly surprised to find a huge mound of posts stacked at the place where they'd quit work yesterday.

He caught Mon Dieu's eye. "Soon's they've wolfed down that bait Ventoso's fixin', have a couple of the boys get those sticks moved out along the line; what's the matter?" he said, eyeing the Frenchman's scowl, traipsing after him as Mon Dieu went over for a closer look. "What kinda wood's this?" the straw boss asked, picking up a post and hefting it, "ain't got the weight of a pint of good bourbon!"

"Tamarisk," Gill said. "Light to handle an' strong as iron. It will heavy up quick once that sun gets to work on it."

"Won't hold the staples," Mon Dieu objected. "It'll split—"

"It'll hold 'em long as we give a damn about. C'mon, let's eat those goddamn frijoles before that muttonhead burns them up!"

"I t'ink he boils hees sock in dat coffee."

"Puts hair between your toes," Gill remarked; but his grin disappeared when they hunkered on boot heels to dig into the refried beans Ventoso dumped in their plates. "Where's that other hand of yours, Vasco?"

"Musta gone back of a bush someplace."

Gill went on with his eating, but when he moved over to drop his plate in the wreck pan and the missing *vaquero* still hadn't turned up, Gill beckoned Whiskery Bill. "How many Del Sol *caballos* you count?"

The Yaqui held up three fingers, and Gill grimly nodded. He took a hard look around and gave the Indian a rifle with the terse comment, "Keep an eye out for squalls."

"You t'ink hees skedaddled?" asked Mon Dieu with a great belch of breath.

Gill was looking at Vasco. "Five'll get you ten he's off on a errand. We're going to have Rivas in our hair before long." He scrubbed at damp cheeks. "Let's get some posts down."

Just before noon, with another half mile of fence firmly anchored, Gill, straightening up to mop the sweat off his face, found the *hacendado* suspiciously eyeing him from the back of a horse some ten feet away. It was plain from his look the man had a bone to pick, and the tone of his voice left no doubt of this at all. "Where'd them tamarisk posts come from?"

Gill said easily, "Found 'em piled up here when I come out this mornin'. Reckon the birds must've dropped 'em like they did with that manna Moses passed round to the children of Israel. While they ain't exactly the sort I'd of ordered, it sure beats havin' to go out and cut 'em."

"That kinda wood only grows on Bar 7!"

"That a fact?"

Rivas said through his teeth, from a livid face: "I want to know what you're doing with Bar 7 posts!"

"Should think you could see I'm putting 'em into your fence."

"Take them out! I don't want them!"

"No one asked what you wanted." Gill said quietly, "No one gives a damn, either. When I set posts they're in there to stay."

Rivas cried, staring angrily: "I don't want no truck with that outfit—you hear me?" And Gill, about to walk off, turned around to say bluntly, "Nothing in your contract says I got to use particular posts. Ain't nothin' there either says I can't use whatever comes handy. You're payin' for whatever my 'services' call for. Now get out of my hair an' go read that thing before you pop off again."

Gill knocked off for lunch and, after he had eaten, told Ventoso to cook something up for the men. "I'll send 'em back here in shifts."

Mon Dieu was one of the last to get fed and came back looking like hell wouldn't have him. He came stomping up to Gill in a fine shine of lather. "That stew ain't hardly fit for a Injun! Judgin' from what I got that sonofabitch musta throwed in everything but the horns an' hide! An' you know what he done when I was fixin' t' tell 'im? Grabbed up a cleaver! Tol' me, by God, t' swaller an' git!"

"Expect he ain't got over his mad at the job yet. If he don't do better pretty soon I'll have a word with him."

"If he keeps puttin' all that sody in hees biscuits—an' that *coffee!* Damn stuff's strong enough t' float a wedge!"

The sun bore down, and heat boiled off the rocks and sand in wriggly waves that turned eyes bloodshot and tempers savage; but when they knocked off at about 6:30 another taut half mile of fence stood behind them and the bawling of cattle piling up against it went on and on, until Gill, trying to sleep, was pretty near minded to shoot them himself.

He couldn't say when it quit but he realized why as soon as he got out of his shakedown and threw off his tarp. His stare, swinging naturally for a look at the fence, spied a half mile of posts, standing bare as a row of bald-headed bartenders. All three strands of wire, when they finally came on them, had been dragged off and left a couple of miles away in a tangle not even Job from the Scriptures could have managed to unravel.

In a fine show of outrage Gill sought out Vasco. "An where were you when all this was goin' on? Strummin' your guitar? I told you to keep an eye on that wire!"

"Jesus an' Baltazar—"

"You can tell that to Rivas! Go tell him, by God, what they've done to his fence! I oughta charge Del Sol double for every inch I do over!"

## XVII

REB LOCKHART drove up with a wagonload of posts just after Mon Dieu's mule skinners finished stretching and fastening the last strand of wire across the vandalized section denuded during the night. He got some hard looks from Vasco but called unperturbedly across to Gill: "Where you want these?"

Gill pointed south. "End of the fence. Drop 'em off about a rod apart till you get to where the river quits. Whatever's left, pile 'em up right there."

The Bar 7 ramrod said, "Del Sol land don't run that far south."

"No skin off my nose," Gill answered. "When I sell fence I put it where the buyer wants it."

"What's he goin' to do with the rest of these posts?"

"Hang wire on 'em. We've still got three miles of fence to put up after leaving the river."

"What's the idea of that?"

Gill shrugged. "Long as he pays for it I don't give a damn. One more load ought to just about do it. You want I should give you the money for 'em now?"

"You can settle with the boss after we've fetched that next load," Lockhart said, turning his head to see where Vasco had got to. But the man hadn't moved and the Texan, apparently thinking better of whatever impulse he'd been about to give way to, tightened his mouth and went driving off toward the fence's far end.

He was still in sight when Rivas, at the head of a huddle of horsebackers, came pounding out of a low line of hills. "You reckon," Mon Dieu said back of his hand, "our friend in the wagon pulled down that wire?"

Gill shook his head. "Got all he can tend to cuttin' them posts. Ain't got enough help on that spread to do both."

Rivas came up in a broil of dust, setting his horse back hard on its haunches. He looked mad enough to burst his surcingle. "What's this I'm told about you charging double—"

"Whatever it is, you heard wrong," Gill said. "All you owe

for this new stretch of fence is just what you're payin' for every foot I put up."

"Baltazar said—"

"Since when is Baltazar runnin' this crew? If you'd put some reliable hands on this job instead of the culls you sent over here to gamble and sleep away—"

"This is Bar 7's work! You can send them your bill!"

"Now just a dang minute. You got a right to be riled," Gill conceded, "but don't take it out on me an' Bar 7. Lockhart just drove off with a load of posts his boys cut up for us, and he sure wasn't up half the night cuttin' wire."

"It's *their* damn cattle went through that fence!"

"I'll not dispute that. We spent half yesterday pushing 'em back. This fence line separates your range from theirs. Only natural there'd be more of their stock than any other kind."

"I want a word with that woman!" Rivas cried, glaring, in no way mollified by Gill's attempt to pour oil on troubled waters. Waving a beckoning hand at his half-Indian crew, he was about to take off when Gill clamped a hand on the black stallion's bridle. "Could be powder burnt, you go rammin' over there in that kind of temper."

"*Dios!* You think I will take this thing layin' down?"

"You'd be smarter to make sure first whatever you figure to dish out is damn well aimed at the parties responsible. You might also remind yourself," Gill said, "if that woman should happen to step into a bullet you could easy wind 'up with a rope round your windpipe."

It had all the earmarks of good breath wasted.

Balefully snarling, the *hacendado* at the head of his outfit went tearing off across the flats at a headlong gallop, bound pretty obviously for Bar 7 headquarters.

Gill peered at Mon Dieu. "Think we ought to go over there?"

The Frenchman shrugged.

Gill scrubbed a hand across the give of damp bristles. But in the end he shrugged, too, and set off with his crew after Lockhart's wagon.

They had not been more than ten minutes en route when a dark silhouette at the mouth of a draw caused the Frenchman to reach out and tap Gill's shoulder. "Over there by the end of that cliff." He pointed. And Gill, following his stare, scrinched his eyes against the sun, took a long hard look and disgustedly swore.

"Where you t'ink that feller he's come from?"

Gill, pushing his glance along the line of the draw, distinguishable for perhaps half a mile by the present pattern of light and shadow, growled, "Looks like he might have come past Bar 7 . . ."

"An' w'at you t'ink he's doing there now, eh?"

"Havin' himself a look at that fence."

"So?"

Clapping spurs to his horse, Gill raced to come even with him, but by the time they got over there the fellow had cut his string and ducked into some hideyhole or hauled his freight. A study of the draw's sand and shale bottom rather suggested departure. Gill said testily, "I'm getting just a little fed up with that geezer."

"You t'ink these Jingo, he's cut that wire?"

"I wouldn't put it past him, though damn if I can see any profit in it for him."

"Mebbe he's work for Bar 7."

"They ain't got the moolah to interest his kind. Though he might, I suppose, be working for some of these half-ass outfits. With Rivas threatening to shut off their water, they might of scraped up enough between 'em to . . . But that ain't the way Sneed tells it; he said straight out nobody knows *what* that hard nose is up to."

"These Sneed, he's mebbe not tell all he knows."

"And that whippoorwill might be here on his own, lookin' to get folks so het up with their feudin' he could waltz out of here with both pockets filled. He *could* be back of this alleged rustlin' caper," Gill said; and then, impatiently: "Hell with 'im! We better get back to stringin' that wire."

They saw no more of Don Miguel and his rifle wavers but midway through the afternoon's stint, with the sun burning down ten degrees hotter than the back log of hell, a dust whipped out of the rimrocks behind them and sped toward the fence like mail being carried through war paint country. Even Gill looked a mite uneasy as the whole crew turned to watch its approach. "Looks like Lockhart," somebody said, and Gill straightened up to rest a hand on his gun butt.

It *was* the Bar 7 foreman, no doubt about it, and the way he was flogging his horse made it seem pretty certain he wasn't dropping by just to hear his head rattle.

The Crockett ramrod pulled up his lathered mount to sit with face working, hands balled into fists, while he heaved and gulped like he had done the running instead of the trembling horse. Gill reached up a canteen to the fellow and, after pouring about half of it into his system, Lockhart, coming up for air again, snarled, "That sonofabitch Rivas!" and went into a spate of cursing that described the Spaniard's ancestry clean back through Darwin to the time when, according to him, they were no more than squiggles in the black oozing matter at the bottom of some forgotten sea.

When he finally ran out of hyperbole and was scraping rock bottom for some further invective, Gill cut in to ask what the trouble was and Lockhart nearly climbed down his throat.

"Trouble!" he shouted. "That swivel-eyed son of a she-goat's miscarriage set *fire* to our place! An' that ain't the half of it! Shot up ever'thing that come in their sights! Kilt our best bull, crippled three horses I left in the day pen; an' if I hadn't got back in time to pull Hallie out, she'd of burnt up inside there like ever'thing else!"

"You saw this?" Gill asked, "saw Rivas himself?"

"Course I saw him! Sonofabitch chased me halfway here!" and he whipped back a hand, with the horse flinching under him, to run a stiffened finger alongside an angry red furrow where the beast had lost hair. "Three inches higher an' I wouldn't of made it!"

"But the woman—" Gill exclaimed.

"Hank and the others is lookin' after her. "There'll be no more post cuttin'; an' while we're on the subject you can pay up right now for them we delivered."

Gill, peeling several bills from his roll of expense money, asked, "She get burnt pretty bad?"

"Not so's you could tell; singed some is all, whilst I was gettin' her out. But if I hadn't smelled smoke an' been near as I was, she'd probably gone up with all her belongin's!"

Gill could see the fellow had blood in his eye. "Guess

you ought to know who jumped you, but that ain't hardly proof they set the fire or done the rest of that stuff."

"Don't mealymouth me with that kinda guff! I know what I seen! Hallie Crockett can count all the enemies she's got on one goddamn finger! An' his names is *Rivas!*"

"What about them beaus her old man run off?"

With an irascible downward chop of the hand, the gangling Texan swept this aside. "Wouldn't none of 'em do a thing like that—why, without Bar 7 standin' up for them there wouldn't be no small spreads in this country! That sonofabitch would have 'em *all* under his iron! When they hear about him makin' war on women we'll have every two-bitter in this county behind us!"

"Maybe," Gill said, "but before you get into this over your ears it might be a good notion to take Hallie in to stay at Quarls's store. Kind of talk you're spreading could get someone killed. I've seen it. I've been there before."

But Lockhart said fiercely, "Just gimme that money! Don't try to tell me how to stomp snakes!"

## XVIII

Mon Dieu grumbled, "Why you not tell about these Jingo? Mebbeso he's one set fire, keel stock."

"You saw how far my talk got with him. Nothin' but the hole left by a lead plum is going to get Rivas out of his craw!" Gill pawed at his cheeks. "You get on with the fence. I'm goin' over there. No sense lettin' Hallie get killed along with him."

Mon Dieu scrubbed his jaw, took a pull at his nose before, with some firmness, shutting his mouth. When Gill got that look on his mug, folks with the barest lick of mule savvy kept their notions to themselves. He waved the crew back to work, muttering under his breath.

Gill stopped by the wagon to pick up his other horse before heading out on the trek to Bar 7. Things certainly looked fixed to boil up a storm and, while this might be grist for his mill, a handy lever for the sale of more wire, he was not uproariously happy.

He tried to persuade himself again that the Crockett

woman's problems were no skin off his butt, but the look of her stayed in his mind just the same—and the persistence of this bothered him.

He couldn't understand it. She was a lot of woman, no two ways about that; but so was Jude Jackson and a heap more his sort.

He guessed a man couldn't help feeling sorry for the way, all her life, Hallie Crockett appeared to have faced hard luck. First in the matter of the beaus her father had discouraged; enough, he reckoned, to have soured any female. Nor had she been luckier in inheriting for range boss a Texican as adamant and prejudiced as Lockhart. But now to lose her home and what keepsakes she'd treasured, on top of being stuck with a grasping neighbor determined, apparently, to force her out of the only way she could make a living was a little bit much for anyone to stomach.

But Judith Jackson, too, in peonage to a fat slob like Quarls, certainly hadn't any easy row to hoe.

Gill tried to look at it objectively, but that did not get him any further. He guessed he must be going soft in the head to be putting any female's welfare ahead of his own, with all the signs and signal smokes heralding what could only wind up as a full-scale corpse and cartridge occasion, tempers being what they were around here. Any guy with the sense to pound sand down a rat hole would mind his own business, make what profit he could and dig for the tules while the way was still open!

Mon Dieu might not have been too far off in suggesting it was Jingo who had set this ball rolling. From the way it looked, the man had been past there; and if he was minded to stir up a fracas, he could hunt a long while for a quicker way to do it. Lockhart had certainly been right about one thing. There might not be any stampede to line up with Bar 7, yet what had happened at the Crockett place would sure as hell open up a fine can of worms.

Violence inspires violence—call it by whatever name suits you. A lot of these jaspers, hanging onto ground they couldn't make a living from, would find in the Bar 7 shindig license for any skulduggery their wits could lay hold of.

Gill shook his head and hauled Rivas back into the focus of these cogitations. Had the *hacendado* taken the bit in his jaws, gone over there and perpetrated the atrocities Lockhart accused him of? Or, Gill couldn't help wondering, would the responsibility, the onus of that aggression, fasten itself to him by virtue of his declared intention and the ironic coincidence of having been near enough the scene of this outrage to accost and throw lead at the Bar 7 boss?

Rivas would be stuck with the blame either way. This was going to get worse before it got any better.

Yet with his mind's eye, Gill kept seeing Jingo's sneer, the hard tight lips in that sweat-streaked face, the skimmed milk stare above tobacco-stained teeth. It didn't need any crystal ball to catch the stink of powdersmoke on him. "Hard case" was written all over that fellow, with his cauliflower ear and slovenly garb, shirt hanging open clean down to his navel. And the more Gill considered the look of him, the more he felt minded to doubt that all the tension and hatred could be laid at Rivas's door.

He thought it might pay a man to keep an eye on that drifter, yet pushing this round, he was not particularly inclined to take off the time for such a project himself. Let some of the toes being stepped on look after it: that fireeating Lockhart, or Rivas himself.

When he got within sight of Bar 7 headquarters, Gill could see Lockhart had not unduly embellished his report so far, at least, as damages went. Charred embers still smoldered with an acrid stench. The house was a total loss, barn, too; though oddly enough the boars' nest—local parlance for an outfit's bunkhouse—remained relatively unscathed, only a corner of its roof lost to sparks. It was inside this building, a blanket wrapped round her, that he found Hallie Crocket.

Somewhat paler of cheek, a bit pinched round the nostrils, she showed none of the hysteria one might have expected. When she sat up to put a hand out in greeting, the ordeal she'd been through, as far as Gill could make out, seemed not to have left any noticeable mark on her.

"So good of you to come," she said, with that hint of intimacy he uncomfortably remembered. She reached up to poke at her hair, rather wanly smiling as those great pansy eyes peered up into his face. A warmer cadence crept into the husky sound of her words as she wound them around him like a spell; and then, shaking her head in its golden halo: "I can't let you take any men off your fence—we'll manage somehow. The good Lord will provide, if one has faith enough . . ."

"Yeah. Well, I'll drop by again, first chance I get," Gill remarked, a bit uncertain how to bring up what he'd come here to say with Hank looking on from the door where he leaned with both fists folded over a rifle. "Might be a good idea," Gill said, gruffly clearing his throat, "to have someone keep a peeled eye on that Jingo."

"You think he's working for Del Sol?" Hallie asked, looking prettily astonished.

"Haven't picked up no sign pointing that way. You catch a look at any of that bunch?"

Miss Crockett shook her head. "I didn't see anyone at all. It was the smell of woodsmoke first caught my notice. I was looking around, trying to see where it came from, when bullets started banging into the walls. There was a lot of yipping and yelling outside, and suddenly everything was smoke and flames. I suppose I panicked. It all seems so confused when . . ."

"You recognize any of the voices?"

"I'm afraid not."

"Understand you lost a—" Gill gulped and said, "some stock," remembering no gent would use the word "bull" in front of a woman.

"We did. Some horses we had in the day pen were shot —and our herd sire. Reb told me someone had cut its throat."

Gill felt uncomfortable the way she was eyeing him. *Weighing,* he guessed, would fit that look considerably closer. She said in a by-the-way sort of tone, "He says he'll see we're paid for them."

"Talk's cheap. Without proof and no evidence—"

"But Reb *saw* them!"

"By 'them' I presume you mean a handful of jaspers riding Del Sol horses. Since he didn't see them here, it ain't hardly likely that is going to be enough."

"He saw Rivas *himself!*"

"So he told me. Be a mite hard to show any connection between them fellers chasing him and what happened here."

"Who else would do such a thing?"

Gill shook his head. "If you're smart, you'll get out of here; you mightn't be so lucky next time. Until this is finished, you'll be a lot safer at the Crossing with Quarls. He can make room for you—"

Hallie Crockett said, with a lift of the chin, "My place is here. I don't intend to lose this spread by not being round when the chips are down. I don't believe Rivas wants it badly enough to do me bodily harm, if that's what—"

"Ain't you forgetting that, except for Lockhart coming by when—"

"I'd have gotten out. This whole thing was deliberately staged. It got out of hand when that wind came up. Rivas, I'm sure, was just making a point, figuring to give me a fright. Probably hoping I'd do the very thing you've suggested, pull out. If he had really been trying to get me killed . . . But he wouldn't," she said, head up, smiling at something not visible to Gill, briskly saying with more confidence, "I've know Don Mike too well to believe that. Oh, he's capable of taking Bar 7 away from me, or, failing that, smashing it; but it's preposterous to think he would ever dream of hurting me."

Gill left without voicing what he thought about that.

## XIX

HE MARVELED how a woman could be so obtuse.

Nothing he'd turned up in his relationship with Rivas inclined Gill to trust that hard-jawed *hacendado* any farther than he could fling a porcupine by its whiskers. Things being as they were, and after what Quarles claimed Hallie's old man had told Rivas, current events at Bar 7 seemed to fit hand in glove with Gill's own private conception of the Del Sol owner's character and proclivities.

Who else around here was half as likely to burn her out? Who else had a quarter of the reasons Rivas certainly must have? Faced with the prospect of paying again for a full half mile of pulled down fence was more than enough to make any cowman go on the prod—especially after seeing Bar 7 cattle gobbling up grass he'd presumably set aside for winter feed. And one must remember that the man's prime intention with this fence in the first place was to keep outside brands—Hallie's in particular—away from the life-giving wetness of that river.

All this, of course, did not rule Jingo out, but made him the less likely cause of Hallie's loss. It wasn't that you couldn't make a case against the drifter, but that, in the role called for, Don Miguel would almost have to be the odds-on choice of anyone conversant with the evidence. Besides having the most obvious reasons, he'd been seen in the vicinity after quitting the fence crew filled with fury and squarely pointed for the Crockett headquarters.

Despite all this, Gill found himself loathe to give up entirely the picture of Jingo sitting his horse at the head of that draw. So much so, in fact, that the first thing he did after returning to camp was break out a fresh mount and go back to the place where he'd seen the man last. And this time, by dint of much looking and a great deal of patience, he backtracked the man to within a hundred yards of the hoof-churned area surrounding the scene of the Bar 7 fire.

Lockhart, spotting him, caught up a horse and came riding out.

Gill said to his frowning inspection, "You see Jingo today?" and got a firm head shake. "Well, he was past here this evenin'. Came to look at the fence. I've just tracked him back here."

Lockhart looked hard at him. "For a guy as anxious as you to git fence up, I don't quite savvy this sudden interest in Jingo. So he come past this place. What the hell of it?"

"May have been him put the match to your place."

Lockhart's snort held incredulous astonishment. His whole face curled derisively. "You won't get far sellin' that notion here. I been around a fortnight or two, an' the only trouble this spread ever got came straight from Del Sol, same as this dido they fetched us today. Why the devil you think them buggers was chasin' me? I'd *seen* 'em, *that's* why! They was doing their damnedest to make sure I'd be in no shape to file charges!"

"Could be," Gill nodded. "It was just an idea I thought you might find some use for."

"You tend to your knittin' an' I'll tend to mine."

When Gill continued eyeing him without remark, Lockhart grumped, "Now I'll give *you* somethin' to grind up with your tobacco. From here on out this spread won't be healthy for varmints eatin' off the same plate with Rivas—an' that includes fence stringers!"

Gill said, as though he hadn't caught up with that last: "To what saint do you attribute gettin' clear of them fellers?"

"Didn't no saints come into it. Turned out I was mounted on a lot fresher horse."

"Still . . . with all that shootin' don't it seem kind of odd not one of them whistlers even give you a scratch?"

"Git," Lockhart grated, "afore I do you a hurt!"

The first person to come under Gill's narrowed stare when he got back to camp was the old he-coon of Del Sol himself, Rivas in person, and with his crew lolling round stowing away Ventoso's eatables with all the sangfroid of permanent boarders.

"Evenin', *patrón*," Gill said dryly. "Thought you'd be home an' tucked between sheets by this time of night."

"We're staying right here until you get this job finished."

Turning this over, Gill got off his horse and took Rivas aside. "Shakes a man up, don't it? Sort of figured you'd show better sense after jawin' I give you this noon. You been almighty lucky. If that—"

He let the rest go to peer at Rivas more closely, given pause by the man's look of bafflement. Either Rivas was a consumate actor or the astonishment Gill saw looking back at him was a heap too real to be dismissed with a shrug. "Mean to say you ain't been near Bar 7?"

In a tone of puzzlement, Rivas said, "I been looking at cows all afternoon." Then, more roughly, "What are you getting at?"

"You was pointed that way when you tore out of here."

"I was pretty damn riled. Couldn't trust myself to talk to her then; we went on across to check up on some critters we been doctoring for screw worm. Now what's all this about?"

Gill told him, Rivas listening like a man in a daze. "*Sangre de Cristo!*" he finally exclaimed. "We were never any closer than five miles of that place. And they think this was *my* work? Hallie surely knows me better than that!"

It was a first rate performance. Pretty nearly tempted to believe him, Gill said, "Got any proof of this?"

Rivas shrugged. "None, I'm afraid, that would stand up in court. These people were with me the whole afternoon, but that won't count for much with you Anglos." The men looked worried and, behind that, angry. He chewed at a lip, eyes searching Gill's face. "Who could have done such a thing?"

"That's somethin', I reckon, you better find out. This ain't going to set at all well with your neighbors." Gill said after a moment, " 'Fraid I gave you a bum steer about that guy Jingo being a deputy marshal. He was over here this noon at the mouth of that draw, havin' a look at your fence. Took off when I rode over there. I backtracked him later practically into the Crockett yard. Maybe you ought to keep an eye on that feller."

"I will," the Spaniard grimly declared, and went off to speak to a number of his men, three of whom presently mounted up and departed.

Gill went over to the wagon, filled a tin plate with a heaping portion of Ventoso's inevitable refried frijoles, reflecting that if he ate much more of this fare, he'd be apt to come down with spontaneous combustion.

Hunkered on boot heels, plate on knees, he watched the trio of *vaqueros* ride out of camp, thoughtfully listening to the fading run of hooves. He didn't honestly know what to think about Rivas; it was, of course, barely possible the man had told the truth when claiming he'd been no nearer Bar 7 than he'd come en route to inspecting those cattle. If secret guilt lurked behind those grim looks, it was well and deeply hidden.

If the man had been telling the truth about his whereabouts, about the only face left that might comfortably fit the role of chief villain was that of Jingo, the hard-bitten drifter who seemed ever to be lurking where chance of action appeared most imminent.

He might have any number of quite valid reasons for being in that draw at the time Gill had seen him. Or he could, on the other hand, quite as well have come straight from that attack on Bar 7.

Hallie claimed to have heard voices yipping and yelling. But one man could easily sound like a dozen if such was the goal he had in mind. One man could have handled that deal very neatly with Bar 7 off post chopping, and Lockhart gone with his load to the fence. You would think if there'd been more Hallie couldn't have helped seeing one of them, or one of their horses. Her not having done so tended to suggest Rivas's story might be true.

But of course, with such a piddling amount of information to go on, Rivas's story could be true and still leave him behind those hectic moments at Bar 7. He could have delegated that skulduggery—they could *both* be involved, if Jingo, by any chance, was in Rivas's pay!

Next morning, Rivas deployed his *vaqueros* to various points overlooking operations—all but the three he'd sent off last night to, presumably, get a line on Jingo's activities. Ventoso was left in camp to look after the stores and fry up another noon meal of pinto beans and sowbelly with plenty of chili stirred in to make sure the stuff would not turn cold before reaching its ultimate destination. Not, Gill reflected, that this appeared at all likely.

Before rejoining Mon Dieu and his muleteers at the fence, he reminded himself to ask if the *hacendado* had pulled his whole crew away from headquarters.

Rivas thoughtfully gave this frowning attention.

"I left no *vaqueros*, but you need not concern yourself on this score. There are *escopeteros* and *hombres muy bravo* to look out for my interests. Do not fear for Del Sol; for more than two hundred years it has withstood all comers."

It may have been the way Rivas put this, the pride and patronage reflected in his tone, which prodded Gill's sardonic wit. "Just one big happy family, eh?"

"Yes," Rivas answered, "I suppose one might say this. A very loyal breed, these old family retainers." He shook his head sadly. "A tradition, alas, all too seldom encountered in the youth of today."

## XX

By NOON, Gill's wire had got to the place where the river's brown water dived into the thirsty sands and disappeared. After his mule skinners had been pried from cook's fodder, they took the fence another four rods before bending it sharply toward Del Sol.

"How far off your line are we setting these posts?" Gill asked Rivas presently, and the rancher shrugged. "Who keeps track of such details? When my father came into his inheritance, Del Sol stretched almost two days' ride in every direction from the seat of his holdings. Rather late in life he developed an unhappy fever—a malady of the dice, one might say. In pursuit of this hobby he gambled away sundry chunks of my patrimony. The exact boundaries, I'm afraid, have gotten somewhat mixed up."

"Give a guess," Gill said grumpily.

"Not over half a mile."

"Who adjoins you here?"

"No one of consequence. One of the rabble who've been eating my steers; a fellow, I think, by the name of Cartrell. Runs eight or ten head which he never looks after, living, he claims, off the 'natural increase.' The man, to be blunt, is a goddamn rustler."

"Whereabouts is his shack?"

"I've never seen it. To know about. Like some of his *compadres* he may live in a cave," Rivas answered with curling lip.

"If you fence him out he's going to squawk, isn't he?"

"Nothin new about that. Most of his life, I would think, has been spent complaining about one thing or another. He's the ruffian I ran out of Quarls's bar the day you came into this *gringo* paradise."

"He could be a damn nuisance."

"No argument there. Some people appear to thrive on misery. Cartrell, I don't believe, could be comfortable without a reed of injustice to lean on."

"Why don't you buy him out and get rid of him?"

"I've already offered. He called it 'oppression.' The 'heel of the mighty' never gets off his neck."

"A ride at the end of a rope," Gill said, "will sometimes work wonders."

"I've promised him that; told him he'll dangle first time I catch him with one of my steers. He's put it around that Del Sol's trying to 'frame' him."

Judith Jackson, Quarls's bound girl, rode up to the fence on a sidesaddled gelding about the time Gill got the next batch of posts set and was scowlingly contemplating having to lay off the next day and take his whole crew to chop out some more. He shelved this prospect to dredge up a smile for her. "What brings you so far from the old man's wing? Surprised the old hen would let you out of the coop," he hailed, striding over to where she sat listening to Mon Dieu's unabashed compliments.

This got no laugh out of Judith Jackson. "It little behooves you," she declared with chin up, "to flaunt your contempt for a man who has stepped so far in your behalf beyond what he figures are the dictates of safety."

"I stand reproved," Gill grinned. "Now what has Mister Quarls, at considerable risk, done in my behalf that has got you into such a fine show of lather?"

"If you're going to make a joke of it—"

"You know," Gill said, "when you get riled, you're prettier'n a speckled pup under a red wagon. With yellow wheels!" he tucked on admiringly.

Eyes flashing, the girl spun her mount and would almost certainly have left forthwith had Gill not reached out a preventive hand. "Hold on—" he growled with a tightening grip. "Looks like I got off on the wrong foot, ma'am—one of my many, maybe worst, bad habits. If we can start out afresh, I solemnly promise to pay close attention. Now, can a man speak any fairer than that?"

With stare uncertainly rummaging his face, the girl finally said, "He thinks you should know, there are two men looking for you at the store."

Gill rasped a hand along his unshaven jaw. "You see 'em?"

She nodded.

"Ever see 'em before?"

She gave him a head shake, and Mon Dieu swapped looks with him before Gill said, "Sure of that, are you?"

"We don't get many of their kind around here."

Gill's glance turned thoughtful. "That kind, eh?"

"Quarls thinks they're killers. Leastways, he says they're packing a grudge."

Letting go of her horse, Gill picked up his reins. "Maybe you better stick around till I get back—"

"I'll string along," Mon Dieu cut in, wheeling to head for where the loose mules were held. But Gill stopped him short. "They didn't ask for you. Much obliged," he nodded, touching hat in Jude's direction, and took off at a lope, in no mood for argument.

He hadn't gone half a mile when a drumming of hooves pulled him round in the saddle to find the girl hurrying after him. He swore under his breath and, when she came up, grumbled, "Thought I told you to stay put till I got back."

"I'm not under your orders."

Gill sank the steel but the girl was well mounted and it was soon evident he wasn't going to outrun her. Eyeing her sourly, he pulled the gelding to a walk.

Without conversation, they covered three miles. Then Gill puffed out his cheeks and said to her irritably, "What did these fellers look like?"

"Plenty *malo*," she answered. "About as hard looking a pair as I've ever encountered—and that's saying considerable."

"That the best you can do?"

"One of them had a bad scar on his neck, could have been an old rope burn," she amplified, watching him. "About five foot four, sort of paunchy round the middle. Wears burnsides and chin whiskers. Other fellow has buck teeth and a gimp. Clean shaven. Ugly. About six foot. Both dressed like townies."

"Yeah," Gill said to the look in her eyes. "When we get there you keep out of the way. Be a good time for you to go take a bath."

"I don't need a bath."

"Go take one anyway. Could turn out to be shootin'. I don't want you underfoot."

"You always get what you want?"

Tone grim, he said, "One way or another."

Night fell early from an overcast sky, and it was fully dark when Gill picked up the lights of Quinn's Crossing. "Reckon they know you took off to find me?"

"I doubt it. Quarls was taking up most of their attention when I slipped away. Seems to me they'd have followed if they'd suspected I was fixing to pass you the word."

Gill, knowing them better, wasn't at all sure of that. But they'd have added up the score when the hours piled up without further view of the only thing in skirts Quinn's Crossing had to offer. It was a pretty sure bet they were waiting right now to get in their licks soon's he got within gun range and, ransacking memory, it seemed altogether likely they'd set it up to have him stopped a good piece before he'd get any help from the gun on his hip.

It had been a lot slower catching up than he'd expected when a man was as brimful of venom as the one bird had been when he'd left him in custody of the law back at Brady; he'd about decided the ropeburned one had been swung as scheduled, and marveled again at the scrapes a man can get into over the bulge in a shirt front, when coupled with a roving eye and a predilection to ignore the regulation of double harness.

When Gill had bumped into Rosie, he'd had no idea that the toast of the Peso Pinto had been hitched to a wedding ring. He'd only discovered this when one night, having failed to show up for work, the girl had been found manhandled and strangled and then tucked lovingly into the bed she'd promiscuously shared with husband Jack Ronstadt, employed as stage driver on the run between San Angelo and Lampasas. Because the job had been tailored to catch Gill as fall guy, he'd been compelled to turn up this Ronstadt as killer. What it looked like now was that the man had got clear and figured, with help, to even the score.

Gill waited by the foot of the waterfall several long minutes after the girl, reluctantly, had gone off into the dark by herself. And while he sat there, dourly wrapped in his thoughts, one sprocket of his mind turned up a notion he could not lightly disregard. Just suppose, for instance, in setting this up, Jack had been cute enough to ring in the girl?

One might deem it pretty farfetched for a stranger to bait his tray with a frail he had never laid eyes on before and who, by all logic, would be hostile to his plan. Yet he could easily use Jude without her knowing it; and the more Gill pushed this around, the more it seemed to him Ronstadt had done just that. The fellow was too devious to have let Jude out of his sight, unless it was deliberate.

So he must have wanted Gill warned.

And even that made a kind of sense when you remembered the bother he had been to at Brady to set Gill up for the killing of that two-timing Rosie.

He must have guessed in the light of previous knowledge that Gill wasn't the kind to run from a bind. So the girl had been used and now it was working out just as intended, with Gill coming in to brace this pair.

## XXI

THERE HAD TO BE a joker tucked into this someplace.

Why would Ronstadt want Gill warned?

Rolling that round in his head, the only advantage Gill could come up with from where Jack sat was that, by this method, Ronstadt could avoid any premature exposure and conduct this shoot-out on grounds of his choosing.

The spider and the fly.

Yet from Ronstadt's view there'd be an additional bonus, accruing from placing Gill in the role of aggressor. Wily Jack was figuring—if anything went wrong—to cop a plea of self-defense.

Gill nodded. That scissor-bill had all the angles covered—all but the one that was going to trip him up.

With a cold grin, Gill got out of the saddle. Having thoroughly sized up the deficiencies and, conversely, the possibilities inherent in his surroundings, he turned the horse loose on dangling reins. Wading out among the river boulders, he selected one inclined to his purpose, only barely removed from the splash of falling water, and sat himself down with considerable confidence to sardonically await the result of this maneuver.

Much of Jack's satisfaction was due for a jolt when Jude turned up, as she eventually would, unaccompanied by Ronstadt's projected victim. As more time passed, still with no sign of Gill, cagey Jack was going to start getting worried, come down with the jitters. It stood to reason he'd be distinctly uneasy when presently Gill's mount, becoming impatient, showed up in town, reins dragging, at Quarls's stable.

That riderless horse was going to play hell with him.

The same curiosity that killed the cat would tug him out of his cover. He might resist for a while and hang fire, swearing, but sooner or later the need to know was going to start both men searching.

Gill didn't ask himself where they would look. If they had half the wits God gave to a gopher, they were just about bound to backtrack the horse.

With an Indian's patience Gill set himself to wait.

One hour dragged by and half of another before the horse, peering at him, commenced reproachfully to whicker. Gill remained motionless through another twenty minutes while the horse pawed the ground. Casting round for fodder, it drifted presently over to make a meal off bushes that were scattered along the bank. Then, as Gill had reckoned, the gelding remembered those good tasty oats it had been fed at the livery and, head high to keep dangling reins from underfoot, took off for town.

Gill stretched out, pistol in hand, to lie at full length on the rock's inclined surface, hat removed, keeping an eye on the trail across the boulder's weathered rim.

In the next two hours he very nearly went to sleep. Twice the rough contact of chin against rock fetched him out of a doze. On the second occasion it occurred to him the pair were hardly likely to come hunting tracks with a goddamn lantern. Nor would they come scratching matches, they'd be thinking too much of their hides to try that. He guessed they would probably wait around for daylight. By which time, he reckoned, they'd be jumpy as crickets.

To keep from getting in the same fix he somewhat reluctantly closed his eyes. But, no longer fighting it, sleep perversely chose to ignore him.

He tried counting sheep and other old wives' remedies, to little avail; yet somewhere along in the small hours of darkness he must have dropped off because the next thing he knew they were out there with rifles in the predawn mists, stares stabbing each covert as they inched their way toward him, following the sign left by Gill's departed gelding.

Quiet as stalking Apaches, both men came afoot, hunched over their weapons, nervous as rabbits, ears stretched, nostrils flared, fingers wickedly hooked about triggers.

Sweat cracked through the pores of Gill's skin but he held thoroughly still, not following their progress lest the pull of his scrutiny act as a magnet to tug their attention. There was nothing he could do in the face of those rifles until the gelding's tracks led them within range of his pistol.

When he judged it was time, he risked another look but they were upwards, still, of a hundred yards away. He wanted to see the whites of their eyes, for if his first shot missed he might never get a second.

Ronstadt was perhaps twenty feet to the east of his companion and at least half that distance closer to the unseen target they were hunting.

It was hard, bitter hard, for a man to lay back grinding his teeth while that pokey second bastard hauled himself into range. Gill had to exercise almost all his will power with the sweat hanging jiggly above half-shut eyes to keep from squeezing off a premature shot.

The fellow kept stopping, peering every which way with the nervousness of a bitch about to drop her first litter. And the hell of it was Jack Ronstadt, stronger of stomach or, perhaps, with more prodding him, kept right on coming. He was scarcely ten feet away from Gill's gun muzzle, staring right toward it, when Gill's first shot knocked the second man sprawling.

Ronstadt fired from the hip, sending rock chips flying in a splatter of fiercely jerked off shots, whose reverberating clamor rose to wild crescendo through screaming ricochets while Gill hugged his boulder to let the frightened silence come creeping back around him.

He could visualize Ronstadt's quandary, not knowing for sure if he'd made the hit or not. Gill let him stew in it, eyes burning with sweat, never moving a muscle until the man's first, cautious, tentative step deliberately rasped the shale underfoot.

Gill, acquainted with that dodge, too, kept grim count of further sidestepping progress until the next stride, he reckoned, must put Jack in sight. Then he lifted the pistol, and Ronstadt, more reckless now, walked straight into it. Gill's single shot taking him square between the eyes.

On his return trip to the fence, through a muggy morning beneath a sky that resembled molten lead, Gill was at no loss for thoughts. He rather wished now he'd checked on Jude, though the innate practicality of Quarls assured him nothing much could have happened under the man's eagle eye and double-barreled Greener. Gill was certainly, at this point, in no kind of shape to be roaming round with anything in skirts!

He wondered if those three Don Miguel had put on Jingo's trail had managed to turn up anything of interest. There likely hadn't been time enough to get a worthwhile line on him. His kind would be holding the cards pretty close to his chest and testing the wind with every turn of the screw. If that trio had any brains at all they would stay out of sight. If they could just keep the bastard under surveillance for three or four days till Gill got the rest of this fence put up . . .

There'd be nothing to hold Gill here after that. Why should he give a damn about these people? He'd come here for a profit, meant to take it and run. No one but a goddamn straight out numbskull would be loony enough to stick his oar into things that didn't concern him. Involvement was for fools and women and ignorant kids still wet behind the ears! Any man with a full set of wheels in his think box soon learned which side of the bread got the butter put on it.

He hoped Mon Dieu had thought to chop out more posts. Might be a good idea, he guessed to get camp moved over onto Rivas's land where, besides being more handy and time saving, a closer watch could be kept on mules and wire. He didn't want any fresh setbacks at this stage.

Rivas, with about half his crew, was just sitting down to another meal of beans when Gill rode in, stone faced, to announce he'd found no one working on the fence and "none of your outfit posted anywhere in sight!"

"Mon Dieu went off with your crew for more posts," the Spaniard said, "and I have six good men keeping tabs on that wire. I've put them up in the hills where they can spot trouble coming before it arrives."

Grunting, Gill took a plate to the fire. Coming back with it loaded, he squatted and blew on his java. "You oughta try Arbuckle sometime, Rivas. Got this slop beat four ways to Christmas."

Don Miguel's teeth flashed. "My *vaqueros* do not have the iron-plated insides the *Señor Dios* gave to Anglos."

With the sun still lost behind a cloud-covered sky, visibility at any distance was something less than reliable to Gill's way of thinking, with the sticky heat building up a haze against that line of quivering hills. He said, with a scowl for the sprawled shapes around him—some half-hidden beneath sombreros, "I'd think your fence would be considerable safer if some of these boys was ridin' line."

The *hacendado's* smile was a goading thing as he put a thin stogie between his jaws. With the weed fired up, he puffed out blue smoke in a series of rings, an unreadable stare playing over Gill's face. "I have been at some pains to encourage these vandals. I should like—with your permission—to catch a few red-handed."

"You've lost me someplace. They could cut that wire and be long gone before your boys could get out of them hills."

"Of course," Rivas said. "Precisely what I had in mind."

Gill stared. "You don't look quite ready for a string of spools. Reckon you've got someone staked out nearer. Those boys up there is just window dressin'."

"Not exactly. I've got a man in that draw where you saw Jingo. If he thinks there's about to be trouble at the fence he sends up a smoke and we climb leather. They'll see us coming and make a break for the hills."

"That way you've got them between two fires." Gill

nodded. "Providing they don't spot the men stashed up there."

"You came through those hills. Did you see anyone?"

"No. But there's somebody comin' hell-bent from 'em now."

Rivas, turning to look, growled some firecracker Spanish and the hands around Gill made a dash for their ponies. Rifles across pommels, they had just returned, mounted, with a held horse for Rivas, when the man from the hills pulled up in a dust hung shower of grit. "There ees smoke at Del Sol!" he cried through cracked lips.

## XXII

IT HAD BECOME through the years a habit, which was virtually tradition, for persons of Spanish extraction never to do anything immediately (save perhaps the gymnastics of courtship) that might comfortably be put off. *"Mañana"* was the Mexican answer to most everything, but there was nothing of tomorrow in Don Miguel's receipt of this startling pronouncement. With a mighty oath, he leaped to the saddle and with spur and quirt took off at full tilt, his *vaqueros* strung after him like the tail to a kite. Even cynical Gill, caught up in the infection of such excitement, climbed back into leather to go pounding along.

In the annals of Santa Cruz county it was far and away the quickest trip recorded. With no concern to spare horseflesh the *hacendado's* headlong pace took them over the miles in far less time than a man would believe; and it wasn't till they were breasting the last ridge that Gill began to feel a distinct uneasiness scratching at the back of his bones, almost like feet tramping over his grave.

At the crest, rimming out, Rivas pulled up to stare, all those behind jamming up in a huddle of bulging eyes and open mouths, braced to witness in the ashes of Del Sol the sort of wild carnage that would make a man puke.

Rivas looked, in his despair and chagrin, as if the bottom had been hacked from his belly, but it was Grudden's drummer who did the swearing.

Smoke still dribbled from the heap of charred embers. Hanging over all was the acrid stench of burnt cloth. He even spied two or three sprawled, motionless bodies in the cotton *pantalóns* which marked them for peons, but Del Sol still stood, every wall and roof intact among the shards of broken out window glass. "Suckered like a bunch of empty-headed fools!"

They could see when they got down there what had made the stinking smoke. All Don Miguel's belongings had been carted from the house, every room stripped bare, and everything piled and burned in the middle of the patio; the loyal retainers he had bragged of lay dead—all four of them shot while attempting to repulse the vanished raiders. Everyone else had been scared off or driven into hiding. Corral poles lay where they'd been yanked from the ground, and, of course, there were no horses.

When Gill, after that first wild burst of cursing, got his wits to working again, he began tramping through the hoof-tracked dust, sorting things out, to emerge at Rivas's side with a reasonably accurate picture. "Seven horsebackers ridin' hell-bent come down on this place like Geronimo's Apaches. No Injuns, though, would of burnt all that stuff; bodies was scalped just before they rode out."

"And who is this 'they'?"

Gill shrugged. "Take your pick. You know these folks a heap better than I do. Tell you one thing, if there's a strand of that wire left tacked to a post, I'll be the most surprised man this side of Chihuahua."

"It's that pig of a *gringo* Texican, Lockhart!" Rivas cried in a teeth-gnashing temper.

Gill shrugged again. "Could be you're right." He scrubbed some of the drip from the end of his chin. "I'd keep an open mind till you've had a report on that snake-eyed Jingo."

Don Miguel cried testily, "I'd have *had* a report if he'd headed this way. Those boys would have got me the word before ever you'd got out of sight of that fence!"

"Well. Maybe so. I guess you'll find out before we get done with this." Gill rubbed at the scraggle of beard on his cheeks. "While we're speakin' of fence, you got enough left in that bank over at Naco to cover restringin' it?"

"Do you think I am loco to put up more fence for those pigs to tear down?"

Gill looked him straight in the eye, grimly nodding. "Yes.

I think you will honor that contract no matter what's been tore down. Unless you want suit brought for damages and a lien clapped onto every acre you own."

Rivas glared.

Gill looked at their mounts. "You any idea where we can get some fresh horses short of roundin' yours up?"

When the man didn't answer Gill, remounting, said, "Reckon I better get back to that wire. You fixin' to stay here?"

The *hacendado* looked pulled two ways, but in the end, darkly scowling, he passed on his orders to one of the *vaqueros* and, muttering blasphemies under his breath, got back in the saddle to follow the tired shuffle of Gill's plodding horse.

"No use killin' 'em," Gill said at last. "If we stop a few hours, we're like to do about as well an' arrive a heap fresher. Speakin' real personal, I'd as soon show up when there's enough light around to get a bead on what I'm up against."

"You think we could run into them?"

"I wouldn't risk ten cents on it; but when you're dealin' with jaspers as het up as them, pays to take a good look at what you're settin' your boot to."

Well before getting his first look at the river, Gill saw the birds. At least a couple of dozen, high up in the blue, were sailing around on outstretched wings, lazily gliding like straws on the wind.

Rivas swore when Gill nudged him. He knew as well as Gill did they were peering at buzzards, and the significance of this was too plain to be doubted. "Bastards have been there, all right," Gill muttered. "I just hope, by God, they left enough of that wire to patch up what they've done to that goddamn fence!"

They kicked up a faster gait from their horses.

A first view of Gill's campsite appeared encouraging. Men were moving about, and mules, standing up, had their heads tucked in nosebags; but the birds were still circling, and when Don Miguel got a look at his fence what he said wasn't learned at his mother's knee.

There were not ten posts in sight still left upright, and

what remained of the wires Gill's crew had put up looked too snarled and mangled to be fit for anything. Cattle of ten or twelve different brands were on Rivas's side of the line, in droves thicker than shelled beans dumped in a sack, and a couple hundred more stood knee-deep in the river.

"How bad is it?" Gill called to Mon Dieu.

The Frenchman growled, "Could be worse—but not much."

"Have they wrecked the whole fence?"

"Haven't looked. Ain't been her more'n half an hour. We got eighteen dead mules an' Ventoso to plant."

Don Miguel's jaws worked, but no words got past the gnashing crunch of his teeth. He had the same kind of look you might see on a bull just before it collapses in the Plaza de Toros.

"What about the rest of that wire you packed in?" Gill asked Mon Dieu.

"Couple of spools been worked over with axes—"

"We got enough, you reckon, to restring the whole fence?"

"Mebbe half," the boss muleteer grunted. "We cut enough posts—" He swung a hand toward the windrows of tangled wire.

Gill reined his mount over for a closer inspection, the Frenchman walking beside him. "Those steers never crossed any mess like that," Gill said, looking across the snarled strands with the uprooted posts sticking out of them grotesquely. "They've come through someplace else. Leave this till we've finished the rest of it. Get the camp moved to where we ran out of posts."

Starting to move off, he said over his shoulder, "Where are the posts you fetched from Del Sol?"

"End of the fence—with Enrique an' his buffalo gun."

Gill found a mile of fence down, and before he reached where they'd started in the lava rocks he counted four other places where the strands had been cut and dragged off to leave hundred foot gaps through which the cattle had been driven onto Del Sol grass.

The camp had been moved by the time he got back, and part of the crew was setting up the new posts, while the rest, ahead of these, were putting down the holes with crowbars and tomato can cups.

"What happened to Rivas?" Gill asked, not seeing him.

"Gone to bring in those mens he had stashed in the hills."

Gill transferred his gear from the horse he'd been using to the one left in camp. "Better pick up those Henrys," he said to the Frenchman, eyeing the rifles Mon Dieu had passed round. "Armin' these boys is just askin' for trouble."

"By gar," Mon Dieu scowled, "them fellers t'row lead, we t'row lead back. You forget Ventoso?"

"We're just doing a job here. It's Del Sol they're after."

"You tell boys that. They not got rifle, you not have crew!"

Gill was too tired to argue. "I'm going to take a whack at following sign. Tell Rivas, when he gets back, there's four more gaps in the fence farther up. If he don't want more of them cows driftin' through he better put men there to turn 'em back."

"Big places?"

"Big enough," Gill growled, and put his horse into motion.

The tracks of the vandals after quitting the fence veered off toward Bar 7, much as Gill had suspected. But these presently surprised him, swinging north into the malpais, where the trail became fragmented as individual riders broke away from the outfit, until eventually he had no sign left to follow. He pushed on anyway, thinking when he reached the far edge of this lava patch to pick up fresh tracks.

It turned out he was wrong; wherever they'd gone they had not come this way. He spent half an hour quartering around until, stumped, he was trying to think what to do next, when the slug from a carbine whined past his cheek, and the horse he was forking went to crow-hopping. By the time he got the brute under control he had no real notion where the shot had been fired from. But a rattle of hooves and one glimpsed blur of motion made him drive in his heels to slam the gelding after what appeared to be a hightailing horsebacker.

Apparently Gill had the better horse, for the fellow pulled up inside a half mile to turn, teeth bared, in considerable agitation.

"Well, Sneed," Gill said, more than somewhat on edge

himself, "you tryin' to put 'bushwhacker' on top of the other things I've heard applied to you?"

"I never fired that shot! As God's my witness . . . Here!" he held out his rifle, butt first. "Look for yourself!"

Gill, sharply watching, passed the gun's breech under his nose, throwing the weapon back disgustedly. "All right. Who did?"

"I've no idea!"

"That just won't wash. When your friends got through playin' hob with that fence they took to the malpais to rub out their tracks. You'd have to be a sight dumber'n you look not to know—"

"Well, I don't!" Sneed said, still appearing half scared but glowering anyway. "I ain't been within three miles of your wire!"

"Then I'll give you some advice. You better dig for the tules an' do it damn quick!"


## XXIII

AFTER LEAVING THE man, Gill did some more looking. Result of this circling materialized when he turned up another set of fresh tracks about a hundred yards from where he'd jumped Sneed from cover.

These didn't tell him a great deal, but he'd plenty of things to mash through his thinker when he got back in the saddle to strike out for camp.

He couldn't help but feel Sneed had, if nothing more, at least a good hunch who had loosed that blue whistler. Sneed may not have been near that fence, but it was dollars to doughnuts he had been with the bunch that had hit Del Sol.

By now Gill had patched up a fairly sharp view of recent events and, recollecting his last talk with Hallie Crockett, felt reasonably sure both the wire cutting and this raid on Rivas was the work of one outfit, a pool made up of disgruntled small owners. Taking this further, he'd have staked a considerable amount that the whole deal, if not actually led by one of them, was the engineered product of either Jingo or Lockhart.

He'd no way of figuring where to come up with Jingo but, thinking to have a good look at Lockhart, once he'd got through the lava rocks he swung toward Bar 7.

He found Hallie still ensconsed in the barracklike building that had been the crew's quarters; it appeared pretty evident there was no one else about. "Where's Lockhart?" Gill growled.

"Off to the Crossing to fetch back supplies." Her pansy stare reflected no pleasure in the way he was eyeing her. She said in that throaty come-hither voice, "Something wrong? You look like the bowl the cat swiped the fish from."

"Depends where you stand, I guess. Fence looks like cheese a pack of rats have been at."

She said, half grinning, "Isn't that what you expected?"

"I didn't expect no bunch of damn fools to pay Del Sol a visit, strip every room an' have themselves a bonfire of the stuff they took out of 'em! Nor I didn't expect to have to look at five stiffs!"

She turned a little pale but declared with her chin up, "You can't have an omelet without breaking eggs. When someone starts shooting, he's apt to be shot back at."

"Where's your crew?"

"I don't think I care for the tone of your voice."

"That's too damn bad." He said again: "Where are they?"

"Strangely enough—in view of your obvious suspicions—they're out doing the work they're drawing down wages for. This happens to be a working cow ranch, Gill. Running a spread of this size short handed leaves little spare time for anyone on it. Which is why I've had to put Reb to hauling groceries."

Horatio Gill was far from satisfied but couldn't see that he'd get anything from bandying words. She wasn't going to admit Bar 7's complicity in any dido involving five shot hombres.

She said, while he stood staring, "I can't see what you're so het up about. You've got a contract with Rivas. Every foot of fence pulled down—"

"Don't waste your breath reminding me of matters I know more about than you do," Gill said harshly in the bluntness of temper. "Just be thinking what you'd do about now if you happened to be standing in Don Miguel's boots." And, touching his hat, he wheeled from the room.

He was more than a little tempted to take a look round and check up on her crew, but in the short stretch of daylight still available, even if they were about, it wasn't too likely he'd be apt to run across them.

He could, if it wasn't so much goddamn bother, ride to Quarls's store and find out whether Lockhart had been by to pick up supplies. But if that was his alibi, he probably had; he could be back of this and never lift a finger. How many generals would you find in front lines?

Anyhow, she was right. Why the hell should *he* care who had pulled that damn raid!

But deep down he did, and acknowledging it was no boon to baffled temper or any balm to the frustrations riding him with the knowledge he'd be immobilized here another week more than likely even if the fence were to escape further damage. And what if Reb Lockhart *wasn't* mixed up with this?

But he couldn't buy that. Not after the burn out they'd had at Bar 7. Who had more reason to hit back than Lockhart? His job was at stake, on top of everything else. And making a bonfire of Rivas's belongings! Who else among that bunch of two-bitters would have the savvy to come up with that?

He started thinking again of that slug whining past him. It was hard to believe it had been fired by Jingo—or any of the others, either. That son of a bitch wouldn't miss three times! Not, anyway, unless he did it on purpose. And that didn't make much sense that Gill could see.

Rejoining Mon Dieu and his muleteers, who were hunkered with heaped plates round a low burning supper fire at the camp's new location, he learned the crew had set forty-eight posts in holes they had dug for the last stretch of fence. "How many more do you figure will finish it?"

"Mebbe hundred an' fifty. We got about half that."

Gill filled a plate and reached for the coffee. "Man at the pot!" three or four of his outfit yelled in unison, and Gill, grinning sourly, went around pouring java. "Who cooked this stuff?" he growled when he'd swabbed the last mouthful onto a half-done saleratus biscuit.

"That friggen Pablo!"

The named man chuckled. "You theenk mebbe I catch job with Meester Rivas? I do better as Ventoso—no?"

"No," Gill said, round the dough in his mouth. "I'll be damned if you do." He said to Mon Dieu, "Rivas back yet?"

"Got back this evenin'. Went off to spread his boys along them breaks."

"How many'd he have?"

"Five—left one out there just in case."

"Who's watchin' the mules?"

"We got 'em hobbled. Reckon we best put a guard out tonight?"

Gill shook his head. "I don't imagine they'll stick their necks out again till we're a heap nearer done." He filled the Frenchman in on his trip through the malpais with passing mention of being shot at, winding up the recital with his stop at Bar 7.

"These Jeengo, he don' like you much."

"You think that hard nose is back of all this?"

"Don' you?"

"I lean more heavy toward Bar 7's ramrod. Don't have to be either of 'em squeezed off that shot. Any of them two-bitters could of done it; reckon they're riled enough about this fence."

Mon Dieu didn't think Hallie Crockett would countenance having her range boss take potshots at Gill, who said with a snort: "Don't suppose he'd tell her, do you?"

"Any woman would know. They can look through man like piece of glass! By gar, I 'member that squaw I have one time up by St. John—"

"Yeah. You told me," Gill said, shutting him off. "Does it make sense to you this Lockhart pelican, given his pet peeves and these sorehead greasy sackers to work on, would sit round twiddlin' his thumbs while Del Sol's fence puts Bar 7 out of business?"

The Frenchman shrugged. "Give us day off we fin' out for you."

"How?" Gill asked, after turning it over.

Mon Dieu's scheme, pared down to bare essentials, envisioned setting the rest of the posts on hand and then, with the mules in tow as though going for more, to go off through the roll of hills on Del Sol, cache the mules and slip back and catch the fence cutters right in the act.

Gill looked dubious. "They won't strike with Rivas's boys on the job."

"Them boys watchin' holes in fence. Be nobody round these end of wire."

While Gill was digging for the bugs in this plan, Don Miguel and three others rode into camp. With Rivas standing in his stirrups to oversee the process, a pair of big-hatted *vaqueros* dragged a third man up to the fire.

"What's this?" Gill hailed, peering at the prisoner who had both wrists lashed behind his back.

"One of the unwashed rabble that's been eating my beef!" Rivas barked. "Cartrell, he calls himself. Caught him prowling round the fence. Take yourself a look at what we found in his pocket."

His arm came up in a tossing gesture. A pair of pliers thudded on the ground at Gill's feet.

## XXIV

CARTRELL'S BLUSTERING denials of complicity were more frantic than convincing. Seeing the disbelief on Gill's face, he cried in a passion of frustrated fright: "I never owned a pair of them things in my life! Sonofabitch planted 'em on me while his peons was tyin' me up!"

Gill, glancing at Rivas's livid cheeks, was not at all sure in his his own mind the Del Sol owner was above such a tactic. This was one of the crowd he suspected not only of eating his beef but of stealing it. And this, on top of what had transpired at his home place, looked enough to push any man into opening avenues for sanctioned reprisals.

Still dubious, he said, "It's your word against his."

Cartrell cried, "Ask Dutch Quarls if Rivas didn't say right in his bar he'd run me out of this country or hang me!"

But Gill knew a man could say a heap of things in anger he'd no intention of carrying out. With the burning stare

108

still fixed on Cartrell, the *hacendado* asked with admirable restraint, "What do you think we'd better do with this dog?"

"We can't just shoot him out of hand," Gill said gruffly. "No matter what he had on him, you didn't actually see him tamperin' with that wire. Might as well turn him loose—"

"To destroy my fence when no one's watching!"

"Well," Gill said, "if you want to prefer charges and take him in to the county seat, I guess you can do it. But you'll never make 'em stick. Bunch he runs with will probably swear on a stack of Bibles he wasn't in miles of your fence tonight."

It seemed pretty self-evident even to Rivas. Bitterly scowling, he told his *vaqueros*, "Let him go," and tossed Cartrell his pistol.

The man picked it up and got onto his horse, jaws tight shut, and went spurring away.

"Hard lines," Gill said. "But necktie parties are going out of fashion, and legally, at least, you ain't got a leg to stand on. You'll get a heap farther givin' him rope to run with."

Don Miguel said nothing, but it was plain his thoughts ran in different channels. It was likely to go hard and be considerably more drastic with the next two-bitter caught with his pants down.

They ran the fence to the end of the line and then came back to put in the patches. Gill told Mon Dieu: "Probably be smarter to leave that big stretch for last. Looks like he's pushed back most of them critters choused through the breaks; take a pretty tough steer to climb through that tangle."

The Frenchman agreed. So they moved what was left of the wire and supplies up to the stretch of torn down fence that was nearest the malpais on the theory that further trouble, if any, was most like to come swooping out of that jumble of black, burnt rock.

Since Gill was himself pretty anxious by now to be off to new deals and more hospitable landscapes, he took over personally bossing the fence crew and put Mon Dieu with a '73 Winchester out in the brush between wire and lava to make sure further visits were not turned loose without heralding.

Don Miguel and his *vaqueros* were still patrolling all places where the fence had been damaged, but Gill felt more comfortable with an anchor to windward. He didn't have to speculate about Mon Dieu.

Though he'd no intention of involving himself in closer communion with either of them, he could not just by willing it entirely keep from his thoughts sundry visions of Hallie or the gamin-faced Judith.

He toyed with the notion of offering Quarls some kind of cash settlement to procure Jude's release, might even have done so had he been at all confident she'd be better off working, as she'd have to, for somebody else. Certainly *he* had no wish to be stuck with the girl!

Too, he considered, more often than he'd have cared to admit, what life might be like with that Hallie around, even going so far on one wild occasion as trying to picture himself in the role of a cowman.

The snort this pulled out of him fetched round the heads and inquiring stares of the two hombres guiding the wire-stretching wheel. Waving them irritably back to their work, he advised himself with more than ordinary vehemence nobody "not a plumb idjit" would crave to latch onto that amount of headaches. He had troubles enough selling wire and putting fence up to last one feller for the rest of his natural!

Women! By Tophet, if a man had to have one to warm the backs of his legs of a night he would be a sight smarter to do like Mon Dieu and pick up one of them moccasined fillies that a man could send back if she got on his nerves!

And while this conclusion still was fluttering butterflylike against the screen of Gill's mind, who should come riding up tto the wire on a workhorse-chested, white-tailed palomino but Lockhart's boss, throaty-voiced, little Miss Crockett herself.

In divided buckskin skirt tightly clasping hips and thighs, and the cornflower blue of a silk shirtwaist setting off her proportions to disturbing advantage, she made a picture of vigorous health and good will that effectively suspended all work on the fence.

"Just thought I should pay you a neighborly call," she remarked with a bright little smile, her big eyes roving all over Gill, "and see for myself what's been putting my foreman's nose out of joint." Then, her look beyond him, "Why are you doing this stretch of fence over?"

One of the pair on the wheel loosed a half-strangled cough but red faced tore into his work with real "new broom" zeal, when Gill's frosty stare raked across his countenance. The man's companion, too, put his shoulder into it, while the fellow with the hammer began driving staples with an uncommon zest.

Gill said to Miss Crockett, "Haven't you heard about these night-flying herons that come flappin' round to sharpen their bills on new barbed wire? We've had quite a plague of 'em in these parts, but I look for it to ease off some now that we've got a bounty put on them. Fifty dollars a head for a few minutes' work ought to get them thinned out in a pretty sharp fashion."

Switching the subject with estimable composure, Miss Crockett allowed she'd come by to "apologize for my rudeness on the occasion of your last visit, Mr. Gill. I'm afraid I lost my temper. It was truly inexcusable considering how highly I value your good opinion and the friendly interest motivating your queries."

"Why, that's mighty big of you, ma'am. 'Fraid we ain't none of us up to our best in this kind of weather. Does it stay this hot round here all summer?"

"Not as a rule. If we could just get a rain!"

"Yeah. Couple good gullywashers would cool off a lot of things. How's Lockhart takin' to those new duties?"

"He's bearing up. The mining people are putting on a hoe down for their help at Helvetia, Saturday night—public's invited. Thought perhaps you might care to look in and meet—"

"Well, thank you kindly. I'm afraid not, ma'am. This fence takes a heap of lookin' after come nightfall, it seems like. And there's that bounty money; I figure to get me a pretty good chunk of it next time them herons come flappin' this way."

Their eyes met and locked, Hallie's purple ones hinting all manner of exciting possibilities, none of which Gill appeared of a mind to apply for. His sardonic stare watched brightening color wash into her cheeks past the tightening smile, as he said, "It ain't that I wouldn't go in a minute if I had my druthers, but we been too long on this job already. Might be as much as my connection is worth to be off trippin' the light fantastic if it happened this wire should get chewed up again." He produced a tired grin. "I'm real sorry, ma'am. Some other time, maybe."

"Yes. We really must," Hallie said, wrinkling her nose at him. "And do come by if you find that you can. The latch-string will always be out at Bar 7."

Gill shook his head as he watched her ride off. She really was an eye-filling woman. Few years ago he'd have jumped at the chance to get her off on a lark like that hoe down, but too much of the nonsense had got baked out of him for Gill to imagine she'd come over here with that cat and mouse offer just for the pleasure of fending him off her. What she wanted deep down in her marrow was to get him out of the way long enough for Reb and his buddies to smash this fence hell west and crooked!

It was too damn bad a nice girl like her . . .

Gill shook his head again and got back to work.

## XXV

But something happened in the late afternoon, along about the time Gill's crew was fixing to knock off for supper, which caused him to wonder if he might not have reached some rather hasty conclusions with regard to Miss Crockett and what was back of her visit.

Jingo rode up to where the victuals were cooking, got himself asked down and was comfortably ensconced on a log by the fire when Gill and the fence stringers showed up for grub. Tradition demanded he be offered a plate, and his gall was such that he mockingly accepted, obviously enjoying how little he was welcome.

"I hear," Gill said, truculently offensive, "you're not above hobnobbin' with some of that bunch Don Miguel calls rustlers."

"Talk's cheap," Jingo offered with no sign of being ruffled. "If a man was the kind to snap up every rumor," he tacked on with a grin, "one might get the idea you got something to hide behind that chip on your shoulder."

"Say what you're gettin' at," Gill growled thinly.

But Jingo, grinning, gave him the unanswerable Latin shrug.

"Already said it." The pale eyes mocked Gill. "You got a mite more edge to your reach than I figured." He picked up plate and eating tools to fetch himself over and hunker on boot heels beside Grudden's drummer. "Who told you," he grumbled from the side of his mouth, "I was a deputy U. S. marshal?"

"Are you?"

"Beside the point. Give somethin' to know where you got that notion."

"Well . . . gracious," Gill drawled with his half-asleep look, rummaging the cant of that hard-bitten face. "Guess it must of been one of them birds that hop round whisperin' into folks' ears. Same one, possibly, tipped me off you been flittin' round back of pillar an' post brewin' up confabs with that Mexkin hatin' Lockhart hombre."

"You *have* been busy. And what did this bird say we been discussin'?"

That skimmed milk stare looked as unreadable as granite. It occurred to Gill he was chinning with a man who would no more care about clobbering a fellow than he would about finding a few stones amongst his beans. A very rough customer—*hombre malo* in the chili eaters' lingo.

He returned Jingo's shrug, even smiling a little as he sardonically hinted, "Seems to me there was some mention of Rivas and this fence I been buildin'."

"Be uncommon strange if there wasn't. Whole country's been jawin' about Rivas and this wire."

"Like enough," Gill agreed. "Price you pay for progress. But there ain't that many been trying to tear it down," he said, with a look fully as grainy as the one he was getting.

"I see," Jingo nodded. "You've got it into your head I'm back of that someplace."

"Ain't made up my mind. But I can tell you this. When and if I decide you have got a part in it, you better be long gone, unless that tough hombre look you been wavin' around has a heap more behind it than just plain bluff."

Jingo laughed. "You're a real card, Gill."

"Pretty good with a gun, too," Gill assured him quietly.

After the man had cleared out, Gill sent Mon Dieu off to find Don Miguel and, when Rivas showed up with the Frenchman a couple of hours later, told him, "You might's well pull off those boys you sent to keep tabs on that whippoorwill. Waitin' ain't going to put no salt on our porridge."

Mon Dieu asked, "What about that idea I mentioned?"

"If Don Miguel here will fetch over the rest of his outfit, all that aren't crippled or can't fork a horse, I think we can get to the bottom of this. There's a lot of loose talk but damn few backin' it up to the point where they're willin' to stop a lead plum for their notions." He considered the Spaniard with an oblique stare.

"Six, maybe eight; most of 'em two-bitters. Probably Sneed for one. That Cartrell, possibly; with Lockhart likely figurin' the angles; and Jingo—paid from a kitty chipped into by all of 'em—furnishing the muscle. Or it could be the other way around, I suppose. Pin the deadwood on them two, you've got no more trouble."

"An' how we do these?" Mon Dieu inquired.

Gill turned to Rivas. "How many horsebackers can you put into it?"

The rancher stared at his boots for a while. "Dozen or so, maybe two, three more."

"That ought to be plenty with my crew. How soon can you have them here?"

"This side of sunup if I decide to string along. But I'll have to know first what sort of Anglo trick you're up to," Don Miguel said flatly.

Gill shook his head. "I'll bend over backwards to be obligin', but a secret shared ain't much of a secret. We might not get another shot at this; when we move, by grab, it's got to be sudden if we're to catch 'em off balance. I don't want to spill no more blood than we have to."

Rivas said, "Something tells me I ought to keep out of this. Every time I've took cards it's cost me money."

"Stay out," Gill said bluntly, "and what you lose could hurt worse'n money."

Rivas rubbed at his jaw. "I thought cash was the ultimate thing with you *gringos.*"

"Expect I had that comin'" Gill growled, "but it don't change the facts. Long as you're round you'll pay for this fence, an' every extry wire I stretch from here out is goin' to cost you double. If you're not available the company'll take it out of your estate. You won't be around long if you don't settle this now."

Don Miguel did not look like this kind of talk sat very well with him, but Gill's was the only help he could count on and, plainly reluctant, he jerked his head in a nod. "I'll have the men here."

Gill got his rope and went after a mule. While he was putting his gear on the critter, he told Mon Dieu, "When his nibs gets back with them hands, if I ain't here you spread about ten of 'em along this fence. With your boys an' what's left of his, kind of sift around casual like and see if you can turn up them night ridin' sons. If you can't, then the way I look at this, the only chance left is to start payin' visits to that bunch of two-bitters an' round up every guy you find packin' pliers."

Mon Dieu said irascibly, "That could get kind of sticky."

"Not if you keep your wits about you. You got to move sudden; get the drop on them bastards."

"An' what'll you be doin'?"

Gill shook his head and picked up a rifle, one of the heavier .45-90s that would knock a bull down, or anything else that got in his way. He got onto the mule and rode off through the dark.

It was not for the purpose of keeping it secret that he had not answered the Frenchman's query. He had no goal in mind when he mounted that mule. Too restless to sit there and wait on Rivas's *vaqueros,* he felt he had to be up and doing, even if it were only poking around.

This deal was narrowing down toward the finish. Too many good men he had known in the past were no longer around because they'd gotten careless or taken too much for granted. When one dealt with people of Jingo's caliber—or Lockhart's for that matter—one moment's inattention was all that was needed to drop a man into an early grave. One miscalculation or overlooked detail and a feller'd never know what the hell had banged into him.

He had not deliberately set out for Bar 7, but it was in that vicinity he presently wound up, still dissatisfied, still filled with an unease he could not pin down. He had to get those fool women out of his head!

Wasn't it just barely possible, eyeing this thing coldly, that Don Miguel Rivas was a lot sharper cookie than anyone had imagined? You could hardly deny it would suit him to be rid of these contentious, small spread *gringos* cluttering up his landscape and outlook, most of them relatively new to this country, shiftless, cross-grained and probably —as he'd been quick to declare—living off his beef; and not above stealing it when opportunity offered.

It probably still wasn't right to shut off their access to water, but this was the way of the world as Gill knew it, indelibly belonging to those brash enough to make their weight felt.

Who was to say the man was too good a Christian to go a step further and tear down his own fence, burn up his furniture or anything else which would reasonably excuse fighting back in kind, using the advantage of his much larger crew to come down on those misfits like the side of a mountain?

It was a cattleman's way to ride roughshod when things didn't suit him. And it wasn't proven yet he hadn't *started* this burning.

## XXVI

GILL WAS TUGGED two ways.

On circumstantial evidence, at least as good a case could be made out against Lockhart, with his pet peeves and prejudice, his presumed loyalty to the outfit and the fact that with Hallie he had a job which might not accrue to him if forced to seek other employment.

Against Jingo, Gill had absolutely nothing but the kind of antipathy naturally stemming from a confrontation between two persons with contrary notions, or a couple of "experts" in the same line of work. There was nothing but the fellow's unexplained presence to hook him into what was happening here, and no more—except by hearsay—could he be paired off with any principal or faction.

Wasn't it Sneed, himself suspect, who had put around the story of Jingo secretly meeting the Crockett ramrod? The man had neither affirmed nor denied this when Gill had suggestively charged him with it. There had certainly been no sign of it bothering him . . . which, again, was no proof Jingo wasn't in this up to his ears.

The only chance Gill could see for putting the responsibility for those gunned down hombres where it really belonged and folding up the cards before this deal got any worse was to catch one or another of them red-handed. And, with this thought in mind, he turned the mule toward what remained of the Bar 7 buildings, to pause yet again as a new notion struck him.

Sneed! Phil Sneed with his thick-lensed glasses and that bit of hide with the worked over brand which—had he not fetched it round to show at Quarls's store—could have made him out a rustler! By publicly calling attention to it, he'd taken most of the fire out . . . He could even have altered that brand himself with just this thought at the back of his mind. And wasn't it Sneed who'd passed along most of the slants Gill had on this business? The rumors and hearsay which had tended to focus Gill's attention on others?

He scrubbed at the scraggly feel of his jaw.

Was Sneed the one who'd been steering this deal? The man didn't have much to lose but a life already in jeopardy if one could believe what he'd said about Rivas. The same ambitious, unscrupulous greed, alongside envy, could be charged against Sneed that Gill had figured to be motivating Jingo when he'd tried to see that bugger as culprit.

A very old pattern, invariably reliable, given the push of brashness and wit. More or less the same tempting guff which, festering in him, had driven that feller Cain against Abel.

Gill wondered if he could prove those spectacles a prop; what would the puny little misfit Easterner would do if somebody suddenly jerked them away from him . . .

He was nearly minded to ride over there. Perhaps he would have, had Lockhart not loomed so much more promising. Lockhart *did* hate Mexicans bitterly and just as fiercely resented Rivas shutting off that water which Bar 7 had to have to stay in business. His job was at stake and, for all Gill knew, the man could be setting his cap for Hallie Crockett. The burning of Bar 7 headquarters could have been in his case, the final straw. And if Gill found Jingo hanging around or, better yet, the pair of them with their heads together, even a kid in three-cornered pants shouldn't have much difficulty adding *that* up!

He put the mule's head around, drifting him toward the home place of the Crocketts.

And found nobody there. Not even the girl or that rifle-packing hard case who'd come that time with word Hallie wanted him.

There wasn't a smidgen of evidence the place had been abandoned, no sign of any hurried up departure. Gill got back on his mule and sat a while, cogitating. And then he remembered. This was the night of that Helvetia hoe down Hallie had suggestively told him about.

Was that where they'd gone? Or only an excuse to account for their absence and provide opportunity for a piece of night riding intended to settle this once and for all?

But surely, if the fellow were innocent, Lockhart was too shrewd a cowman to leave this place unguarded again. Or did the man think he'd too much to gain to waste help watching a place already gutted?

But if this hunch were right and the woman had gone with them—unless under duress—she had to be a party to whatever it was Lockhart figured to do. Of course, *she* could have gone to that dance in the mountains. And her ramrod, knowing her intention and counting on it, could have reckoned this the best chance he'd get, using it to bring his plans to fruition.

Either way, he would still have had to get help, the Bar 7 crew being too short handed to have encompassed that raid on Rivas's ranch at the same time Del Sol's fence was being wrecked.

Gill decided, after all, to pay Sneed a visit. For if he, too, was gone, a man could just about figure there were other greasy sackers backing Lockhart's game.

So engrossed had Gill become in the leap of thoughts chasing through his noggin, that for once in his career as a despised wire salesman all the stay ropes of caution were allowed to dangle untended. Thus the first inkling he had that others might be jogging this way came with the sudden sharp rasp of shod hoof against stone.

It fetched round his head, sent a hand dropping hipward to freeze, immobilized by the derisive sound of Jingo's chuckle off somewhere in the dark to the left of him.

"Fine time you picked to be caught chasin' moonbeams," the man chided dryly, getting back in the saddle to bring his horse forward. "You're gettin' too careless to stay in this league, Gill. Next thing you hear could be somebody shovelin' dirt on your coffin."

"You must have eyes like a cat," Gill said sourly. "What are you foolin' round in the dark for?"

"Had an idea you'd do just what you did. Visit Bar 7, then head for Sneed's place."

Pushing that round in his head, Gill said thinly, "An' what makes you think I'd be headin' for Sneed's?"

"Nearest of that bunch to Bar 7, ain't he?"

"You goin' in for clairvoyance?"

"Man doesn't need no crystal ball to read your mind."

"Tell me more," Gill said, wishing he could better see that hard-jawed face.

"You've got it in your craw Reb Lockhart's the jigger behind these burnings and what's happened to your fence. You figure he'd need more help than he's got, so you're shiftin' scenery to determine if Phil Sneed's in on it."

Gill was so astonished that instead of saying "Gracious" he broke out with, "By God, that fib I flung at Rivas musta nailed you plumb center!"

"Pretty shrewd guess. I'm down here on orders from the District Court."

Gill said, disgusted, "They got a law out now prohibitin' sale of this newfangled wire?"

"Might be a good idea if they had, judged by the killings it seems to provoke. But that's not in my province. Seems they smelt something fishy at the county seat when a certain party, havin' haunted the listings of recorded sales, began digging into this Del Sol grant. Figured there might be some kind of swindle in the making."

"This 'interested party' try to hire your gun?"

"Bit too cagey for that, I'm afraid."

Gill thought Jingo pretty cagey himself and said, trying to pry some kind of cue from him, "What are you proposin'?"

"Since you appear so bent on turning over stones, thought I might string along and see what you come up with."

"You figure those boys'll be ridin' tonight?"

"Wind seems right." Jingo picked up his reins. "You think Sneed's part of this?"

"Pretty easy led, I'd say."

"And what will you do if we don't find him home?"

"Got a bunch of those Del Sol *vaqueros* strung out along the wire. Rest of them an' my crew under Mon Dieu should be makin' some sweeps tryin' to pin down them rannies. Failin' that, I've told 'em to look in on them small spread outfits an' pick up anyone they find with pliers."

"Ain't that kind of high-handed?"

Gill, thinking of Hallie, said, "You can't make a omelet without breakin' eggs."

"You could pass up the omelet," Jingo growled dryly.

They considered each other. Gill, mouth tighter, said, "Mind if I have a look at that tin?"

Jingo, chuckling, got out his credentials. "You're in the wrong line of work."

"Strike a light."

"Ain't that a little mite risky?"

"Risk an' me is old buddies," Gill said. "Now get out that match if you want to stay healthy."

You could tell by the tone he meant every word of it.

## XXVII

CAREFULLY WATCHING those burly shoulders, Gill could feel that skimmed milk stare like a cold wind blowing across the bridge of his nose. Not at all sure he'd get off first shot if that hunched up shape drove a hand beltward, Gill was damn sure set to give it a try.

Perhaps Jingo sensed this. In any event, the shoulders, relaxing, moved in a shrug. One fist went up to brush the brim of his hat, then both hands cupped the flair of a match.

"All right. Blow it out," Gill said a moment later, passing back badge and wallet.

"I take it you're satisfied?"

"Not really," Gill grunted, "but we'll work on that assumption."

With no further conversation, they rode three miles at an easy jog before a lopsided moon broke through the cloud cover and ten minutes later revealed the unlighted huddle of Sneed's ramshackle buildings.

"Gone to bed, looks like," Jingo said, peering.

"Gone someplace, all right. No broncs in that pen."

Jingo hailed the house but nothing came back. "Has it occurred to you," Gill asked, with eyes still quartering that huddle, "it might be this Sneed that's set off the whole dido?"

"I've checked him out. Nothing we could turn up gives the least indication he's anything more than a stupid pawn. Got his cap set for Hallie."

"He has?" Gill swore. "What the hell does he imagine she could ever see in him?"

"Don't know. Might surprise you to learn he's not the only one."

Gill twisted his head to peer at the man. "All two-bitters?"

"One way of getting help when you're short handed."

"Let's get on with it," Gill growled. "You know where this feller Cartrell hangs out?"

"Yep," Jingo nodded, and put his horse into motion, swinging west; Gill silently followed, one hard thought overshadowing all others.

Jingo, presently pulling up, murmured, "No sound of shooting."

"You expect some?"

"We're only about two miles from Rivas's home place. Kind of figured if any mischief was afoot, that's where we'd likely find it. Rivas ain't the only one been hurtin' for lack of elbowroom. There's a tucked away, brushy draw half a mile from here. That's where Cartrell holes up what time he's not movin' cattle."

"So he *is* a damn cow thief!"

"On a fairly small scale. Too timid to ever get big at it, likely," Jingo said, and got down. "We'll hoof it from here." He hitched his horse to a catclaw. "Have to play this by ear. You follow my lead."

"You think he'll be home?"

"If he is, he'll have company." He struck off through the brush, moving quiet as an Apache, pistol in hand.

Gill's lip curled a little. His old man had taught him never to lift a gun unless he figured to use it, and somehow suddenly, the outlandish idea of a government dick creeping along through the slap and scratch of this godamn brush, a drawn gun in his fist, smacked too much of Nick Carter or that hogwash of Buntline.

It seemed unlikely, it crossed his mind, that a small timer like Cartwell would think to hole up practically under the jaws of the gent he was robbing.

Gill began to feel edgy.

He just couldn't believe any situation they were apt to encounter could be so deadly or hurried up frantic as to make at all logical any precaution as drastic as that.

All the shelved suspicions he had felt about Jingo began to heat up and nip at him again. It would be so easy for the bugger to whirl and recount later, after Gill's mouth was shut, how his gun had got snagged on a branch and gone off.

Marshals, not to mention sheriffs, did sometimes go sour or think to get there faster on income not tied down to a salary. Burt Alvord whose fine sense of humor had turned a mite rough, and that Nevada feller at Alder Gulch came easily to mind.

Although he left his six-shooter tucked where it was in the sheath on his thigh—habit being too ingrained to break—Gill's sharpened stare clung to the man ahead like a leech.

In this fashion, they worked their way up a shallow draw, Jingo after a bit pausing to hold up a hand, beckoning Gill nearer. "Shack's just ahead a couple dozen steps; hear that horse pawin'?"

Gill listened, nodding. "Think they're all here?"

"Not likely. Lockhart probably—might be one other. Main bunch—the understrappers, will be gathering, I reckon, someplace south of us . . . all done by timepiece on a prearranged plan. Good chance here to bust this up if we don't get careless or go off half-cocked. With luck," he murmured, breath fanning Gill's cheek, "those boys with Mon Dieu might just happen to barge into them, or vice versa. I think, on that chance, we'll bide here a spell. Let's move up where we'll have the drop on them. Case our birds take a notion to bolt."

Gill, suspicious, reached a hand to his shoulder as the man half turned in his stride to move off. "If this Cartrell's so dinky, what in Tophet would Lockhart come *here* for?"

"Why not wait, you mean, with the rest of his outfit? Don't know. Got me stumped; don't make sense, but he's done it twice. Might be they've got some deal on the fire that's nothing to do with the rest of this business."

"If you been here twice before one of them raids, why the hell didn't you stop 'em?"

Gill could feel Jingo's stare through the moon-dappled dark. "I'm not lookin' for minnows," he gruffed, bluntly curt, and pulled out of Gill's grasp.

Warily watchful, Gill followed, making nothing at all of that last piece of gab. On two other occasions, by his own admission, Jingo'd had this place under observation and never lifted a finger to apprehend Lockhart or anyone else. Yet now, he'd said, it was time to move in and bust the play up. How had Lockhart changed? Or was something else different?

Only thing Gill could hit on was his own presence here, the implications of which got a pretty close scrutiny. Was it him? Was *he* the big fish that burly ape wanted? Had the whoppy-jawed fool teamed him up with Reb Lockhart!

## XXVIII

SURE LOOKED THAT way, he couldn't help thinking. Yet common sense, harking back through the miles they'd come over, could not help demanding if such were the case, why come out *here* to drop the fact on him? Why hadn't the man collared him as soon as he'd gotten that gun out of leather?

Did he figure to catch the two of them together? Had the man been too canny, or afraid, to tackle Gill head-on, hoping in confusion to bolster his chances?

That didn't add up. With both of them in gun range Jingo cut his luck in half.

Gill shook his head, never taking his eyes off the shapes ahead. If not Gill, who *did* the man suspect, if, as implied, he counted Lockhart a minnow?

Who else was there?

Ahead of him, the man with the marshal's badge stopped once again to put out his hand.

Gill closed cautiously, every muscle cocked to grab iron at the first hint of duplicity.

Jingo beckoned, pointing. Peering through the dark tangle of branches Gill saw before them a moonlit clearing, some seventy feet at its widest diameter, at the far side of which a packing crate shanty with one glassless window hole drunkenly leaned against the thorny growth behind.

A tow sack was hung across this single eye giving the look of a slumbering cyclops; but lamplight filtering round the ill-fitting door suggested—as did the three hitched horses off to one side—the place was not untenanted.

It seemed to Gill uncanny the way Jingo managed with such apparent ease to put a finger on facts. Made one wonder how he'd known three people would be found here. In the night's loamy quiet a mumble of voice sounds came over the clearing, but no separate words Gill was able to distinguish.

Leaning toward him Jingo said under his breath, "When they come out of there—no matter what happens, you back my play. You got that?"

Gill said just as blunt, "I'd have to know more than I do right now to take chips in that kind of game."

He could see the shape of Jingo's face tighten and the swell of his chest as the man's eyes dug into him. "I'm not playin' games. This is law business, Gill, and you better remember it!"

"That's *your* story."

"You callin' me a liar?"

"I'm not buyin' no pig in a poke."

"Well, for Chrissake! What does it take to convince you?"

"More than a badge and a handful of paper," Gill said just as quick, "you could of took off some poor bastard's dead body."

For several instants Jingo stared without answer, and Gill, braced for trouble, gave him back tit for tat. "All right," the man breathed harshly, "stay out of it then. Don't get in my way."

Before Gill could frame any comeback to this, the shack's door was flung open and Lockhart strode through the light to move at a purposeful gait toward the horses. The bulkier shape of Cartrell came after him, and Jingo, motionless, crouched in his tracks with no indication of being on the verge of making an arrest.

Gill shot a dark look at him as the Bar 7 boss, latching onto his reins, reached out for a stirrup. As Lockhart lifted to thrust a boot into it, Gill said thinly, "Hold it right there."

"You fiddle footed fool!" Jingo cried, furious, as the lamp went out; something snarled past Gill's cheek, with a gun's blast slamming loud through the babble. Lunging erect, the man's bitter shout called for surrender in the name of the law. "Stop!" he cursed, "or by God I'll drop you!"

A thunder of hooves ripped the welter of sounds and flame lashed lurid from Jingo's piece, as he blindly fired trying to bring the horse down. "Watch yourself," he shouted as the hooves tore on—"one of 'em's out there!" and, whirling, plunged through the clutch of branches, sprinting toward the shack's rear.

A gun opened up as the unmounted man, behind rearing horses, snapped two futile shots in Jingo's direction. Then Gill, caught up in the excitement, yelled: "Grab hold of them horses an' stay where you are!" But it was breath wasted. The man wanted out, and his piece barked again, forcing Gill to drop flat as blue whistlers clipped twigs from the brush where his chest had been.

The moon's light, brighter now that the lamp had been snuffed, enabled Gill from his new position to spot the man's legs. Deriding himself for so quixotic a notion, he nevertheless called: "Throw down that shooter!" and knew by the cursing as a slug cuffed his hat he was dealing with Lockhart, and squeezed off a shot.

The legs disappeared as the Bar 7 boss, yelling, staggered back and went down.

"Throw it out," Gill called, as the terrified horses broke loose and bolted, "or, by God, I'll finish you right there!"

He couldn't see the man now in that hodgepodge of shadows. Another slug came at him, and he fired at the flash, listened through a brief thrashing and finally stood up as the silence crept back.

He was stepping from cover as Jingo, herding someone ahead of him, came round the shack.

Gill stared, not immediately recognizing this slim figure in pants with her hair all tucked up under a hat. When he did, his jaw dropped, and Jingo said testily, "An old friend of yours," swinging her round to the moon's light. "Where's Lockhart?"

Gill, still peering, flung out a hand. "Jesus Christ!" he said, "you gone off your rocker?"

"Not likely." Head canted, the badge packer held up a finger, and Gill faintly heard the pop-popping of rifles. "Sounds like your bunch has caught up with the rest of them. Well, take a good look at her. She's the one back of that wire cuttin' and burning. Like enough back of that cow stealin', likewise, when we get down to it."

"But to burn her own place?" Gill growled, eyeing Hallie.

"Figured, I guess, that would throw folks off—"

"But *why?* I mean, she had a good thing. Why would she . . ."

"In hock to the bank clean up to her eyebrows. Said if she didn't pay up by next month they would have to foreclose, sell her up, bag and baggage."

"I still don't get it. She spoke pretty high of Don Miguel." He said to the woman, "You an' him was sittin' the bag, way I get it—figurin' on double harness till your old man run him off the place."

Her look of contempt with that pulled up chin was all the change Gill could get out of her.

The marshal said: "What a lot of folks thought. But I got it tracked down, put the screws to Sneed. It was *her* put that story around, what her old man was claiming he'd do to Rivas—wasn't a gram of truth in it. Fact is, Rivas just plain up and quit her. What you're seeing is a woman scorned. Even without the bank coming down on her, she'd of gone after Rivas tooth an' toenail . . . just bidin' her time till you come along. It was the fence, I reckon, put the fire under her; she had to move then or be washed up for sure."

**Nelson Nye** was born in Chicago, Illinois. He was educated in schools in Ohio and Massachusetts and attended the Cincinnati Art Academy. His early journalism experience was writing publicity releases and book reviews for the *Cincinnati Times-Star* and the *Buffalo Evening News*. In 1935 he began working as a ranch hand in Texas and California and became an expert on breeding quarter horses on his own ranch outside Tucson, Arizona. Much of this love for horses can be found in exceptional novels such as *Wild Horse Shorty* and *Blood of Kings*. He published his first Western short story in *Thrilling Western* and his first Western novel in 1936. He continued from then on to write prolifically, both under his own name and the bylines Drake C. Denver and Clem Colt. During the Second World War, he served with the U.S. Army Field Artillery. In 1949–1952 he worked as horse editor for *Texas Livestock Journal*. He was one of the founding members of the Western Writers of America in 1953 and served twice as its president. His first Golden Spur Award from the Western Writers of America came to him for best Western reviewer and critic in 1954. In 1958–1962 he was frontier fiction reviewer for the *New York Times Book Review*. His second Golden Spur came for his novel *Long Run*. His virtues as an author of Western fiction include a tremendous sense of authenticity, an ability to keep the pace of a story from ever lagging, and a fecund inventiveness for plot twists and situations. Some of his finest novels have had off-trail protagonists such as *The Barber of Tubac* and both *Not Grass Alone* and *Strawberry Roan* are notable for their outstanding female characters. His books have sold over 50,000,000 copies worldwide and have been translated into the principal European languages. The *Los Angeles Times* once praised him for his "marvelous lingo, salty humor, and real characters." Above all, a Nye Western possesses a vital energy that is both propulsive and persuasive.

T 48883